The Mirror
&
Nine Other Short Stories

T032944·3

Susan Nde Nkwentie

Langaa Research & Publishing CIG
Mankon, Bamenda

Publisher
Langaa RPCIG
Langaa Research & Publishing Common Initiative Group
P.O. Box 902 Mankon
Bamenda
North West Region
Cameroon
Langaagrp@gmail.com
www.langaa-rpcig.net

Distributed in and outside N. America by African Books Collective
orders@africanbookscollective.com
www.africanbookcollective.com

ISBN: 9956-791-55-5

DISCLAIMER
All views expressed in this publication are those of the author and do
not necessarily reflect the views of Langaa RPCIG.

Table of Contents

The Mirror

Christina stood in front of the mirror for the fourth time. She had just taken a bath and was oiling her body. The mirror was her favourite companion when she was oiling her body as it reflected her slim body and she often wondered at the wonder of the human body. She often wondered whether one day she would be like her mother or the other women she had often admired.

She was alone in the house and had come to the parlour to enjoy looking at her body as she rubbed the Vaseline on her stomach and budding breasts in particular. She could only see part of her body, from the knees to her head. The lower part of her body was not visible. She did not mind because that part of her body did not interest her. She could not see her legs because the lower part of the mirror was missing. It had broken off one evening when she had taken it into her room to have a better look at herself. She had thought that her image in the mirror was going to give her some answers to the questions in her head.

It was a family mirror and had hung on that spot since Christina was born. She could not remember any body taking it off the nail on which it hung. It had always been there with its gilded edges painted gold. It hung on the string to which it was attached and maintained a kingly position in the parlour. Everybody came to it for a last assurance before leaving the house.

Father combed his hair there and made sure his tie was in order before he went out to work. He was a messenger at the Delegation of Health in Bamenda. Although his job required him to move from one department to another or run errands into town, he received his salary from government and did not consider it proper for a civil servant to go to work for government without putting on a coat.

Mother also combed her hair and arranged her headscarf in front of the mirror. To the children it was the last spot to stand and hurriedly run a comb through their hair before rushing off to school. It was a routine action because their remained on their skulls like contours on a hillside. It belonged to nobody yet it belonged to everybody. It was one of the things in the parlour apart from the radio set which indicated that there had been better days.

The rain was still falling when Christina and her two younger brothers came back from school. .Although they were wet they had enjoyed the race from school in the drizzling rain. Since nobody stayed at home while they were in school, their mother usually left the keys of the house with their neighbour. Christina went over and collected the keys. She wanted her brothers to take off their shoes before entering the house. As the eldest child and a girl she was responsible for warming up the food their mother usually left for them. After eating her brothers were surprised when she asked them to leave the plates for her to wash. It was their duty to wash the plates. This they usually did quickly looking forward to being allowed to go and play football with the other boys in the neighbourhood. The playground was an empty lot near their house. Today Christina wanted to wash the plates herself. In addition to this strange gesture she told them to go and play football if they wanted to.

It was muddy on the empty lot but the boys enjoyed playing in the mud. The play style was called 'Tombe' which was more interesting as the slipped and fell in a random chase after the ball.

After washing the plates Christina came to watch them play for some time. She just wanted to make sure that they were fully involved in playing before she went back to the house to carry out what was on her mind. She had come back from school that day curious about what the bigger girls had been saying in school. She wanted to verify if what they were saying was true. She had taken off the mirror off the nail on the wall. Five cockroaches escaped to safety into cracks in the wall. A wall gecko scrambled quickly away, stopped, looked around with its pale sightless eyes before disappearing into the rafters. The area the mirror covered was cleaner than the rest of the wall. But Christina did not see all of this. She hurriedly took the mirror into their bedroom. She was intent on satisfying her curiosity before anyone came into the house. Alone in the room she had taken off her dress then her pant. She looked at her body. She examined her budding breasts and felt the nuts inside. She lifted her arms up, one after the other and examined her armpits. She rubbed her pubic mound and pulled at the tiny strands of hair which were making their appearance. She turned round straining her neck to look at her buttocks. She had never been so aware of her body. The mystery of it all still dominated her thoughts.

Partially satisfied with what she had seen, she dressed and took the mirror back to the parlour.

As she stretched her hand to put the string holding the mirror back on the nail, she was distracted and released her hold before the string got to the nail. The mirror came down with a thud. The lower part cracked. Christina screamed. Her brothers came rushing in to see what had happened. She stood terrified. The boys looked with awe at the broken mirror and the cracked section which had fallen off, She tried to put it back but it could stay in place. She could not put the mirror back on the wall because of the loose section that kept falling off. So she placed it by the cupboard. The boys sat by the door waiting. Christina had committed a serious crime and everybody was afraid of what was going to happen. Their mother came back from the farm and passed into the kitchen to keep her basket. She did not go into the parlour. No child came to welcome her. She called 'Christy! Christy! Christina came and stood at the door.

'What are you doing there?' She asked. 'Won't you come and remove the vegetables from the basket? What do you think we will eat this evening?' Christina did not move. The youngest boy who stood by watching to see what Christina was going to do suddenly blurt out.

'She broke the mirror'

'Which mirror?' the mother asked.

'The mirror in the parlour' the boy replied. She rushed to the parlour to see for herself

Oh trouble! Trouble!' She exclaimed. She knew that the evening was going to be stormy when her husband came back. The blame was not going to be on Christina alone but on her as well. When a child did something good it was credited to the father, but when the child did something bad it was the mother who bore the blame. When she returned to the kitchen Christy was no longer standing where she had been. The vegetable was not also in the basket. Christy had taken them and was preparing them some distance away. As soon as her mother appeared she left what she was doing and ran away.

'Come back', the mother called. 'Come back and prepare the vegetables. I am not going to beat you. When your father comes back he will know what to do'

That evening everybody was very quiet and the children very obedient until Papa came back

Christy, who has taken the mirror away? Pa Ngwa had asked as soon as he had entered the parlour. He had glanced at the mirror on his way to his room. Instead of seeing his image in the mirror he had stared at a blank wall.

'Who has taken the mirror away?' he repeated

He never said where is... when he is asking for anything, because he believed that if anything is not where it should be, then someone must have taken it away. He was always forgetting where he had kept his personal effects and would ask.

'Who has taken my shoes? Who has taken my watch?'

Ma Lai, his wife would grumble and ask herself if she wore the shoes with him, the she would reluctantly go and look for them. So somebody must have taken away the mirror. This time he was correct. Christina came stepping quietly into the room as if the sound of her footsteps would aggravate her crime.

'It fell' she answered almost in a whisper. She was standing at the door ready for any eventuality, for she knew what was going to happen after her declaration.

'How did it fall?' he asked as he moved over to feel the nail on which it had hung. The nail was still firm.

'How did it fall? He asked with his voice rising as his temper rose. In the same half whisper she replied. 'I took it off'

'What were you doing with it? He made to grab her. She had been waiting for just this move and dashed outside.

'Come back here or I will kill you today!' he shouted after her

Mami Lai came out of the kitchen wiping her hands on her loincloth.

'Oh this child will one day kill me in this house! Always looking at herself in the mirror as if she is a beauty queen! With her nose like a spear.' She followed her husband into the parlour and lifted the mirror from the floor near the cupboard where Christy has placed it. The lower part fell of and shattered. The sound of breaking glass echoed in the silent house. Pa Ngwa looked at his wife with a deep frown on his face Mami Lai stood confused. She had made the situation worse. She quickly hung the broken mirror back on the wall and withdrew to her kitchen. Though the mirror still served the family, it was never the same again.

Christina was in her place of refuge, a guava tree behind the kitchen. She could hear her mother talking to herself.

'I wonder what she will do when she becomes a woman' Christina was used to hearing her mother talk to herself, but she never really listened to whatever she was saying. She stayed on the tree until such a time that she imagined her father's anger to have cooled down and then she had come back to the house. The six stokes of cane she received on her palms did not dampen her anticipation of the day she would become a woman. She was going to be like the women she had seen in the magazine which Pascaline brought to school. The smile on their faces showed that they had no worries. They must be very rich and famous women to appear in such magazines, she thought.

Last week the Class Seven teacher had caught Pascaline with one of such magazines. He had quietly come upon them in the school garden. The others had run away leaving her with the book in her hands. She was punished for bringing such a magazine to school. The next day during morning assembly a warning was issued to girls from class five to seven not to bring bad magazines to school. The teacher was not explicit but they knew what he was talking about.

Ti was two months to the writing of the Government common Entrance Examinations into secondary schools. The pupils were preoccupied with their studies. The stain of the morning and evening classes was much and Christina forgot about the women in the magazines. The warning, advices, taunts and pleading of their teachers were working on their young minds. The teachers and headmaster of Government Primary School Bamenda were proud of the performance of their pupils.

For three consecutive years they had scored a hundred per cent at the Common Entrance Examination. The headmaster was very proud of his school and never missed any opportunity to remind the pupils that they had to keep the tradition.

At home too the parents were anxious. Pa Ngwa having seen the value of education made sure that his children went to school. But his interest ended at the level of paying their school fees and providing their basic needs. He never asked himself what his children would become. He never talked about their school work with them. His only belief was that they would become something someday if they do not die young. To Pa Ngwa the futile would take care of itself but to Christina she was going to take care of the future. This could only be done first by going to college. Christina had this focus in mind, when during break time one day her concentration was again shattered.

The night before, she had felt a dull ache at her lower abdomen. She did not tell her mother because it was just one of those aches that led to a spontaneous purging, or maybe it was caused by the unripe guavas that she had eaten. In the morning she did not purge and the ache had disappeared. Later on in the day, during break time, she noticed that Pascaline and her friends were not at the dining shed. She wondered where they could have gone to. She went towards a group of girls who were playing 'rounders'. They were not among them. Then she went to the school garden. They were not under the mango tree where they usually sit when they had something to discuss or look at. She stood for some time trying to imagine where they would have gone to. Behind the school toilet! Yes they must be there. She also knew that when these five girls disappeared something must be going on. They were behind the toilet huddled round a magazine. Christina quietly came towards them to have a look. This magazine was not like the others. It was different. It was more interesting than the others. It contained pictures of women with only their under wears and brassieres on. There were women in bikinis. The pictures of the men were more interesting. They had only their under wears on with a distinctive bulge. On other pages the men and women were standing facing and smiling at each other. These pictures were very interesting and Christina gazed at them admiringly. Her admiration bore the edge of mystery because of what the girls were saying. Caroline in particular was most descriptive of what the men and women did. Whether from experience or imagination she gave a vivid description of what goes on.

You see how they are standing' she pointed at a man and woman

'He will stretch out his hand and touch the woman's breast' then he will say 'I love you'. Then he will put his arms around her and embrace her. Then he will put his mouth on hers and kiss her'. The girls laughed. She continued, 'He will ask her whether she loves him' Pascaline interrupted

'Chei Caro, you are talking as if you were there.'

Caroline did not want the attention of the girls to be taken away from what she was saying. She replied 'Yes' before she realised the implication of her answer. Then in anger she said 'I will not tell you anything again.' The girls were disappointed. Pascaline as leader of the group and the one who brought the magazines did not like the attention Caroline was getting. So she said

'If she does not want to tell you, I will' and she continued.

'Then he will take her to his room and open her legs.' There was silence for some time and the girls burst out laughing.

'Sh sh sh' Pascaline silenced them. 'If the teacher comes and catches us again, I will not be punished alone. And I will never bring another magazine to school again.'

'Please tell us' the girls pleaded. Caroline gave Pascaline a warning look. Pascaline blurted out.

'The he puts his penis in her vagina' There was a hushed silence. The girls busted out into laughter. Christian stared at Pascaline. She could not believe what she had heard. She dared a question 'Does it pain? Caroline turned on her. 'Go away, you baby. This is not for babies to hear. You will know when the time comes'

Pascaline closed the magazine and got up. Without looking at the others she started walking away. The session was over. The girls walked away towards their classroom in silence. What they had heard was not a topic for discussion, not now. Christiana did not follow them immediately. She was mystified. The whole story had sounded so... what was

9

there that the girls were hiding from her? She wondered. She was a girl and a woman. What was the difference?

As Christiana sat in class that afternoon, her mind was far away. She wondered whether her mother knew the things Pascaline and Caroline where talking about. Her mother was a woman and had given birth to four children. So she must know such things, but why did she not tell her about them? Why was there so much secrecy in being a woman? Maybe she was still a baby as Caroline had said. She touched her breasts. They were already pushing our\t her uniform which was becoming uncomfortably tight on her chest. Was she ever going to have the experiences they were talking about? She wondered. She turned round to look at Pascaline who was sitting at the back of the class. Their eyes met and Pascaline smiled. She did not understand why Pascaline had smiled at her. She did not return the smile. She did not like what they had talked about behind the toilet and the prospects of being a woman frightened her.

She had once seen a brownish patch of stain on the skirt of Caroline's uniform. She had stood up to answer a question asked by the teacher. Her friends had quickly given her a pullover to tie round her waist covering the stain on her buttocks. That day the bigger girls were whispering and giggling in class. She had heard the word 'menstruation' several times that day. She tried to find out what had happened to Caroline. But they just brushed her questions aside. Caroline had been unusually quiet in class that day. For the rest of the rest of the week she kept to herself, preferring to sit in class rather than go out to play with the others. During these days Christina watched her closely. So much was happening around her. There was so much she had to learn.

Mami Lai was busy preparing the evening meal. She had come back from the farm very tied. It was the weeding season and the weeds were already overshadowing the crops. She had to pull them out before the rains became too heavy. Each evening she needed help and Christina was there to help her. As Mami Lai stirred the fufu corn in the pot, she noticed that Christina was distracted. She was staring into the fire instead of keeping it burning. She had allowed the fire to burn low. This was not good for the fufu would have a loose consistency instead of being elastic.

'What are you thinking about Christy? It looks as if you are worried about something. What is it? Tell me'

Christina looked into her mother's face, then into the flames. She did not know how to ask the questions. She was afraid of being scolded if she asked the question that was upper most in her mind. But she could not let this opportunity pass by.

'What is menstruation, Mami'? Her mother looked at her for a moment. She poured more water on the fufu corn and covered the pot. She kept aside the bamboo stick with which she had been stirring fufu. Her mind was whirling with the question. She was playing for time. She did not know what to say. She had never discussed such things with her own mother, no with any other woman. What was she going to tell her daughter? She wondered. Then she remembered what her mother had told her when she had first experience the flow of bipod.

'It is what makes you a woman.' She replied. Christina stared at her waiting for her to continue, but she did not. She had not told Christina anything new. Men did not menstruate. That she knew. She could not ask further questions for her mother had picked up the bamboo stick, opened the pot and was stirring again. In disappointment Christiana got up and went out.

As Christina sat in class a moth before they were to write the Common Entrance Examination into Secondary Schools she again felt an ache in her lower abdomen but dismissed it. She had had these aches before. Soon she felt warm as if urine was trickling out of her but she did not feel the pressure of urinating. The warmth turned into clamminess between her thighs. The afternoon classes were coming to an end and she waited for it to end so that she should go to the urinary to check up what was causing the dampness. At the end of the class she stood up and one girl sitting behind her exclaimed.

'What is that on your uniform?' Christina turned to look. The same stain that she had seen on Caroline's informs was on hers. She looked at it in confusion. She was tempted to lift up her skirt and find out what was happening to her, but attention was focused on her. The boys were booing and running out of the classroom. The girls were laughing at her. No one offered to tie a pullover round her waist. She stood looking at how her classmates were laughing at her and she felt ashamed. She felt that she had done something terrible or stupid. Tears started flowing down her cheeks. Caroline moved over to her.

'Do not cry Christy. It is a normal thing. Many girls have seen it and they do not cry. You are a real baby' she taunted then continued, 'Remove your pullover and tie round your waist. When you get home remove you underwear and wash it.

This was all the education that Christy had about dealing with menses. She felt frustrated. The teacher had gone to the urinary to ease himself. When he got back some of the girls were still in class.

'What are you still doing here? Get out and let me lock the door!'

Christina did not want to get out of the classroom. She wanted a place to hide. Pascaline and the other girls stood in solidarity around her.

'What is wrong with you girls? Get out!

'One of the boys shouted. 'It is Christy!'

'What is wrong with her? He asked. Then he saw the tears in her eyes and the pullover round her waist and understood. He had seen many girls in such a situation but there was nothing he could do. Even with the pullover round her waist Christina was the last to leave the classroom.

When Christina got home she went into their bedroom and removed her stained uniform. She put on another dress. She took the bundle and was on her way to the bathroom situated beside the kitchen.

'Are we not going to eat today?' Linus, rather younger brother asked.

'Let me wash my uniform first.'

'We are hungry, your uniform can wait'

'You too can wait' she shouted angrily back at him.

'We will go and take it if you do not want to give us.' Okay go and start the fire. Put the soup on it to get hot before you put the spoon in it.'

'But why are you washing your uniform today?' the boy persisted in his questioning. 'It is Monday not Friday or Saturday.'

'I fell down in school, so I have to wash my uniform.'

After cleaning herself up she came back to the house. Soon the clean underwear she had put on was clammy between her thighs. She was afraid to sit down. She did not know what to do. She took underwear and put it on. This too was becoming wet. She stood around waiting for her mother to come back.

Mami Lai was unusually late from the farm that day. After weeding she had gone to fetch some firewood. She came back from the farm with the bundle of firewood on her head. She was very tied and had no wish to start cooking the evening meal. There was some leftover soup and this was going to be enough. She had expected Christina to peel some cocoyam and put them on the fire as she had instructed in the morning. There was nothing on the fire and Christina was nowhere to be found. Christina was leaning on a guava tree behind the kitchen thinking.

'Christy! Christy!' she called. 'Where can this child be?' she wondered. 'She remembers nothing that is told her. There is nothing yet on the fire' she grumbled. Christina heard her voice and left the tree. On her way from the kitchen where she had kept the bundle of firewood, Mami Lai heard footsteps, turned round and saw her.

'Where have you been? Why is the cocoyam not yet on the fire?'

'Mami, I am sick'

'What is wrong with you?' She asked. Christiana did not reply 'Come into the house and tell me' She followed her mother into the house. When Christina told her what had happened, she opened her box, took out a packet of sanitary pads and gave her. 'Use that. When it is finished let me know. You are a woman now', this was all the education she had on dealing with menses. Christina was puzzled. 'A Woman? Was this all that identifies a woman?' she wondered. No! She did not like it. She was not sure that the women she had seen in the magazine with such smiling faces experienced things like this. They were different and she wanted to be like them.

The next day Christina was at the broken mirror. She looked at her breast. They were larger than before. She examined her nipples carefully. They were swollen and tender to the touch. There were some white swellings at the tip of the nipples like white pimples. She tried to squeeze them but nothing came out. She imitated some of the postures of the women she had seen in the magazines. She turned round winked and smiled at her image in the mirror. She was a woman! Then it occurred to her that her mother must have had such an experience too.' Did she menstruate? 'She wondered.

Then she remembered that on certain days her mother came back from the farm and immediately went to the bathroom for a bath and on other days she did not. Many other occasions were rushing into her mind to testify to the fact that her mother menstruated. Christina had once gone into her mother's room and seen a packet like the one she had given her. The puzzle was becoming unravelled.

Christina did not like the type of life her mother lived. She saw other women on her way to and from school. She met them at the market, but she did not know much about their lives as she did that of her mother. Her mother went to the farm almost every day of her life. She had no money of her own. The little she had from selling her crops went into the neighbourhood thrift and loan scheme. When the money is disbursed, much of it went into her husband's hands. Whenever she asked him for money it was the same response, 'I have not paid the children's school fees.'

Her mother was all smiles they day her husband comes home with piece of loincloth for her or clothes for the children. This usually happened before Christmas.

No! Christina wanted to be different. Some of the magazines they had looked at did not have women in the nude. These magazines had pictures and stories about the women. These were successful women, women who had made it in life. Some were medical doctors, university lecturers, business women pharmacists etc. When the other girls were commenting about the women in fashion dresses Christina would think about this women and wonder. She looked forward to being like them one day.

Their class seven teacher always talked about education being the basis of everything in life.' Without a good education you cannot make progress in life'. He was also fond of saying that his pupils will one day pass him by the roadside in their cars and splash muddy water on him. Christina always felt sorry for him when he said this and promised him in her heart that she would always stop and give him a lift. He was such a genial old man who to Christina was more a father than a teacher.

It was the month of May. The Government Common Entrance into secondary schools was just round the corner. The pupils were given extra homework. Christina enjoyed arithmetic. Figures fascinated her and the various combinations in subtractions, multiplication, addition and others like simple interest and compound interest were her favourites. English language was difficult with its tenses, parts of speech, punctuation etc. These all were complicated to her. The other subjects were all going to be combined under General Knowledge. Christy was determined to pass in list A. They were cajoled, warned, punished and praised to get them prepared for this great examination. Late in the evening Christina would sit alone in the parlour studying. From time to time her thoughts would stray from what she was reading and she would wonder at the type of woman she was going to be in the future.

She was impressed by the work of nurses and doctors. She had gone to the hospital many times because of the rashes she always had on her body, which could not be treated externally. A blood test had to be done. She was very frightened when she saw what was going to be done. It was not going to be like an ordinary injection. Rubber tubing was ties round her upper arm until the area around her lower elbow swelled. A needle larger than the one used for injections was inserted into her flesh. She had screamed and her father had held her arm and her whole body firm against his body. After the initial scream from the entrance of the needle into her flesh she had clenched her teeth and covered her eyes. The nurse had spoken so gently and reassuringly that she did not know when it was all over. From that day she had thought it was such a nice, noble and courageous thing to take care of the sick and dying, but she was afraid of corpses. She also admired the nurses in their smart white uniforms. They looked so special. She wanted to be one of them.

The women who spoke on the television always looked so beautiful and well-dressed. They spoke such good English and French. She wanted to be a journalist to be seen and admired by everybody. She also wanted to be a business woman. In their neighbourhood was a shop owned by a woman. The goods there were sold both in bulk and retail. Large trucks came from Douala to supply goods there. There were assorted items like children's tricycles, soft drinks in plastic bottles, flour in bags etc. She had once gone there to buy retailed sugar for one hundred francs and found the woman sitting with stacks of banknotes on table in front of her. She was counting them and a man was putting them in a large envelope. Christina had been fascinated at the sight of so much money and she wondered how she became so rich. What interested her much were the gas bottles used for cooking. She had once followed one of her friends to their house during break time and seen one of such bottles standing in their kitchen. The kitchen was so clean. There was no sign of smoke on the walls or ceiling. She wondered how this was possible, but she was too ashamed to ask.

When she was tired of studying in the nights, she would dread going to bed to sleep because she was sure that her younger brothers had wet the bed. Their room always stank of dry urine in the day and in the naught it had a humid pungent smell. She could not fall asleep because of the wet mattress. Also in the dark the clothes hanging on a rope in their room took on grotesque and frightfully shapes. These frightened her and she always kept her eyes closed as soon as she put off the lights. To drive away her fear she would imagine living in one of the houses she had seen in the magazines, with sets of beautiful chairs, carpets, and window blinds to match. She imagined cooking with on a gas cooker in a smokeless kitchen.

When she finally fell asleep, she had many dreams. One that made her to wake up one night sweating was about the Common Entrance Examination. She had arrived late for the exam and was in a panic. When she was given the question paper she could not understand any of the questions. When she took up her pen to write her name her palm was stiff and sweaty. She could not write anything. When he teacher collecting the scripts of the pupils came to her, she ran out of the room crying. Then she woke up. Her right fingers were still clenched as if she was still holding her pen. Her body was hot and her bladder full. She had to get outside to release the strain both on her bladder and mind. On another night she saw herself on the television screen but she could not hear what she was saying. All these dreams kept her alternating between hope and despair.

Their home was made up of a parlour and two bedrooms. Her parents occupied one of the bedrooms with the youngest child while she shared the other room with the boys. She did not like the cramped condition of the room with the boys wetting the bed and throwing their clothes all over the place.

With the determination of becoming like the women she had seen in the magazines and living in a well-furnished house, Christina passed the common Entrance Examination in list A and was admitted into the Government Bilingual Secondary School Bamenda. From what her father had told her and from words of encouragement from her teachers, Christina was ready to face the challenges of life in this new school.

Two weeks before Christina was to start college she had the flow of blood again. This time it irritated rather than frightened her. She had learnt that sanitary pads were used during menstruation so she asked her mother for money to buy a packet. She thought that her mother was going to ask her questions, but she did not. Three months had passed before she had this flow of blood and had felt relieved but knew that this was not the end. She was better now at handling the situation but hadn't the courage to ask her mother all the questions that were going on in her mind.

Surprisingly, in this new school the girls did not only bring magazines, they talked about it during break time and after school on their way home. Some of them even boasted of having boyfriends 'Boyfriends!' Christina wondered. She remembered that Pascaline had boasted that she had a boyfriend. The whole idea was becoming a puzzle. Christina had thought that it was a nice thing to have a boyfriend from the way the girls talked about them, but it was appearing not to be so. She had witnessed a quarrel between two form three boys and a form four girl. It had happened so unexpectedly. Christina happened to have been standing by this girl in front of the dinning shed as she ate the 'puff puff' she had bought. These two boys had passed by and one of them had said

'Harlot!' The girl turned round and asked.

''Who are you calling harlot?' The boys responded

'You' they pointed at her. Christina was confused. She was not familiar with the word 'harlot and watched to see what was going to happen.

'Did you call me a harlot?' The girl asked.

'Yes' the boys chorused again. They continued.' Do you think that Clement is your boyfriend? He does not want you any more'

'Who is Clement?' The girl asked. 'I do not know what you are talking about. And for your information, I am not a harlot.'

'Yes you are!' The boys chorused again. A small crowd was gathering around them. One of the boys continued.' Do you think we do not know what happened yesterday? If that happens again we are going to deal with you, you harlot.' And they walked away laughing. The girl was too surprised and angry to answer back. She burst into tears. Her friends rallied round her to find out what had happened. In tears she could say nothing and the two boys had disappeared. The story as Christina later heard was that the girl had an upper sixth boy as her boyfriend, but she was too flippant and had gone round boasting to her friends about her boyfriend in the high school. The boy who had wanted to keep the relationship secret was angry when he heard this and had stopped the relationship. The girl had become angry and had thrown abuses at hind each time they met. The boy had also become angry and had sent his two 'small friends' to abuse her. This had resulted in the unexpected exchange of words.

When Christina heard the story she was surprised. If someone does not want to be your friend any more she did not see any problem in that. You simply stopped moving and doing things together. She herself had stopped being friends with so many girls and there was no problem. She understood that making friends with a boy was the same as making friends with a girl. She had seen many girls in her former previous school eating together with boys. She played with her younger brothers at home. They were her friends. She did not see anything wrong with them. But her views were changing with the new knowledge she was getting. She could not understand it all. She could not establish a relationship between having a boyfriend and menstruation. She understood that sex was something between a man and a woman, something that is done in the dark, is hidden but pleasurable, but bad all the same. Imagining the act was beyond her understanding. Soon she also understood that money played a role between boyfriends and girlfriends.

The dinning she of the school could not be compared to the primary school Christina had attended. It was larger and contained a variety of snacks, which the students bought at break time. The centre of attraction was a kiosk set up by Brasseries du Cameroun to sell soft drinks to the students. Not only drinks were sold in this kiosk. There sardine/spaghetti sandwiches, pancakes made with spaghetti and eggs popularly known as 'spaghetti classic'. There were cakes biscuits sweets chocolates etc. In fact the boy selling in this kiosk knew what appealed to the appetite of the students. 'Classics' was very popular and everybody made the effort to get money and eat a plate of it. It was sold at a hundred and fifty francs. It was not only tasty; it distinguished the rich children from the poor ones. A slice of the sandwich and a bottle of coke, sprite, or Fanta were sold at 350 FRS. This was more than Christina's break time money for one week. There were days she brought no money to school having been told to eat properly in the morning.

Christina used to watch the boys and girls who stood round this kiosk with awe as they ate and drank and wondered. She wondered where they gigots all the money to spend on such delicacies. She concluded that they all must come from very rich families. How she envied them. Some of the students indeed came from rich families and were given enough money for their lunch but others got the money from other sources.

It was not uncommon for friendship to be established across the classes. At the age of thirteen and in form one Christina could pass for a form three girl. One day after eating her puff puff for fifty francs she stood watching a girl as she bit into a slice of 'classic'. When the girl noticed how Christina was looking at her, she walked towards her, cut a piece and asked.

'Do you like it?'

'Yes' Christina replied before realising that the girl's question might have been caused by the way she had been looking at her with longing in her eyes. Then she hastily added 'I have already eaten some puff puff.'

The girl said 'Just take it and eat. If you want more I will give you'

'Thank you', Christina relied. 'This is enough' She bit into the slice of 'classic'...the taste of sardine made more saliva to pour into her mouth. She chewed slowly, not wanting to betray her longing for this delicacy to the girl who stood and watched as she ate.

'Thank you', Christina said again after she had swallowed the last piece. She did not like the way the girl had been looking at her and she felt ashamed. She turned to go.

'No, do not go yet.' The girl held her hand.' What is your name? My name is Grace'

'My name is Christina'

'In what class are you?

'I am in Form One A'

'Oh I thought that you are in Form Two. Okay, Christy tomorrow I will be here. If you want to eat 'Classic' meet me here and we will share' Christina was overcome with gratitude and thanked the girl again. At that moment the bell for break over was rung and the students started rushing to their various classes.

Christina lingered outside watching to see into which class Grace was going to enter. She saw Grace walking into the form One D classroom and was surprised at this. She had imagined her to be in form two or three. She sounded so confident of herself. Christina was afraid of making friends with a girl in a class above her, but seeing Grace walk into the D classroom wiped away her fears.

Christina's determination to stick to her books was being derailed by other information which she was getting out of the classroom. These were lessons which only life can teach, and Christina was a fast learner. What her parents did not teach her, her friends did.

During the first term Christina had gone home immediately after school. She helped her mother in preparing the evening meal and shouts from her mother were taken without complain. She was very conscious of everything she did and paid attention to details. She kept her uniform spotless and insisted that those of her younger brothers be clean too. During the weekends she asked her mother what work had to be done at home or on the farm. This she did quickly and returned to her books. Her results at the end of the term were good. She passed on all the subjects.

Mami Lai was impressed with this change in her daughter. She was secretly happy that Christina was growing into a responsible girl. She saw her growing into a matured woman, getting married and getting children. Christina never thought of such things. All she thought of was getting a good education and becoming like the women she had seen in the magazines. She did her homework every evening. She made the effort of answering questions in class and drew the attention of many of her teachers. The school library fascinated her. It was not a big library, but she had never seen so many books in one room before. She wondered what was in all the books found on the several shelves.

She loved reading stories and telling her younger brothers these stories in the evenings. Their teacher in class six and seven had encouraged them to read stories and had provided them with story books. Christina had read *Eze Goes to School*. It struck her that Eze's behaviour on the first day of school resembled that of her youngest brother. When she told them the story she exaggerated and compared her brother Linus to Eze. This had brought on squeals of laughter from the elder of the two brothers and a frown from Linus. They started calling him Eze and it became his nick name.

Presently, in their Literature lessons they were being taught Kenjo Jumbam's *The Whiteman of God*.

Tansa's home village was not different from theirs. Although Pa Ngwa's family lived in town the children often went to the village on weekends and during the holidays. They enjoyed life in the village without its restrictions. The trips to the river to fetch water, the games they played climbing the mango tree behind their grandfather's house, the fights with other children by the riverside, the impression the Catholic Church made on their minds were all found in the text. As Christina told them sections of the story as they were taught in school, the events kept the boys laughing. The teacher had a creative mind and made the story come alive in the minds of the students. This story telling helped Christina in her understanding of the text and she always good marks in Literature though English Language was still the problem.

All of these took place during the first term. Christina met Grace at the beginning of the second term., which was in January. The excitement of Christmas was still lingering in Christina's mind and the month of February was fast approaching. The youth day was approaching. In the primary school preparations for this day gave the school a festive atmosphere. Classes were suspended on the days preceding the youth day for the students for March-Pass-Practice, human investment, games and other competitions to take place. Christina looked forward to see how the youth day preparations were going to look like.

Meanwhile Christina's friendship with Grace increased. They were always together. What actually made the Christina's friendship with Grace to be strong were the delicacies the Grace brought or bought in school. Sometimes she brought some types of biscuits that were not found in the kiosk. She often bought 'classic and a bottle of Fanta or Coca cola which they shared. Christina enjoyed the biscuits especially the ones with the sugary dry paste sandwiching the pieces together. She envied Grace and thought she was a very lucky girl to have parents who gave her so much money to buy such delicacies every day.

Since her first menses, Christina had started noticing that she often had some pain in her lower abdomen that disappeared on its own. On many of such occasions there was no real reason for the pain and she soon forgot about it. On the morning of the tenth of February, Christina felt this pain again. The sharpness of it woke her from sleep and she wondered what was happening. It was five a.m. and she could no longer sleep. Her younger brother in the abandon of sleep had thrown his leg on her. In anger she pushed it aside and got out of bed. She went to the parlour where she had kept her books on the table. She switched on the light and sat down to read. She took out her chemistry exercise book to read the notes she had copied from the board. After a few minutes her mind moved away from 'The Properties of Matter which she was reading. She thought about what Grace had said the day before.

There were no classes on the tenth of February. After the last Match Pass Practice the whole student body was asked to go to the Bamenda Municipal Stadium to watch the finals of the football competition. During the eliminatory matches which had involved all the secondary and technical schools in the sun division, Government Bilingual High School was leading in its group and was to play the finals with Government Technical High School which was leading in its own group.

The finals drew a crowd not only from the students of these schools but also from the population which loved to watch a good game of football. The students of GTHS were already cheering on one side of the pitch before their players made their appearance. Those of GBHS could not be quiet, as this would be a sign of defeat before the match began. So they started singing their own songs. The songs mocked at their opponents and praised their players. The students of GBHS asked their opponents in song to be ready with a big basket in which to carry the goals that will be scored home.

When the players of both sides appeared there was thunderous cheering and the names of the most prodigious and favourite players were called out. The GBHS players were dressed in white while the GTHS players were dressed in red. Amidst loud cheering and boos the District officer took the kick-off and the match started.

Christina had watched football matches on television in their neighbour's house but had never been a spectator at such a big event. She watched with fascination as the ball was passed from player to player, dribbled and scored. She laughed more at the shouts of praises, curses and comments thrown by the spectators at players on both teams and soon she was responding likewise, shouting clapping her hands and stamping her feet in disappointment when their player missed to score a goal. The boys from GBHS were agile and offensive. They had three opportunities to score but missed them all. The first half of the match ended without any team scoring. During the first five minutes of the second half the centre forward of the GBHS team took everyone by surprise by scoring a goal from a remarkable distance. The spectators went wild.

Students rushed into the field, much to the chagrin of the game officials. The match continued with the GTHS team trying valiantly to equalize but that was the lone goal of the match. The victorious students greeted the end of the match with delirious joy. The school authorities present ceremoniously congratulated the players and organized a victory procession through the main street of the town, Commercial Avenue.

Amidst the euphoria at the end of the match, Christina had lost sight of her friend, Grace. At the entrance to the stadium, as she was walking out she felt a hand on her shoulder. She turned round and it was Grace.

'Will you come with me to the market?' Grace asked. 'Remember what I told you. We must go and get money to buy whatever we like tomorrow. Christina then remembered that Grace had told her of the type of delicacies she bought on youth days. She had also said that girls brought a lot of money to the field on that day to buy food with and some even came with as much as two thousand francs. Is Christina wanted she could get some of the money for herself for the next day. When Christina had asked her how she was going to get the money, Grace had told her to wait and see. Grace had also told her that her mother sold garri behind the main market and Christina believed that they were going there to see her. As the jubilant crowd passed them by moving towards City Chemist junction Christina and Grace took the opposite direction to the market. They took a side path which led through the area were women plaited their hair, walked past the area where vegetables are sold and came out on tether tarred road that leads round the market. As they approached Grace pointed out her mother amongst the women who had basins of garri on front of them. She did not even have a stall of her own. She was selling in the open air. Christina wondered if this was the woman who gave Grace all the money she brought to school. If she was then she really loved her daughter.

'Mami, we thought we should come by and see you after the football match before we go home. This is my best friend, Christina. Christina shook hands with her all the time wondering about Grace. There was something wrong. Grace's mother did not look like the type of woman to give her daughter all the money she brought to school or spent on delicacies. Grace continued

'Mami, you know what? Our school won the match. It was one goal to zero. Our team played very well'

'Is that so?' replied the mother.' Then your team must be very strong.'

'Yes mami, the boys played as if they were playing for the World Cup.' The mother laughed.

'Mami, I am hungry.' Grace suddenly changed the topic.

'What do you want me to give you in the market? There is food in the house. Take taxi money and go home. I know that you are tired' She opened her purse took out two hundred francs and gave them. 'Pay one hundred francs each. Go to Mami Ngozi and take the money for the bucket of garri she took yesterday'

'Yes mami, I will not forget' Grace replied as she held Christina's hand to lead her away. They did not return the way by which they had come. Grace led her towards the back entrance of the main market. They passed through the section where meat is sold and came to the section were merchandise is sold. There were rows and rows of assorted items like clothes and shoes for men and women, kitchen utensils accessories for hair decoration ladies' hand bags etc. There were open lanes and closed lanes between the rows of shops. They got to a shop in one of the closed lanes and Grace asked Christina to wait outside while she went inside. She soon called for Christina to join her. A bright bulb that threw bright light on the items in the shop hung from the ceiling. The boy in the shop greeted Christina warmly and she wondered where he had known her. The boy asked her about school and she answered absentmindedly, her eyes staring from one shelf to the other. There were rows and rows of assorted tined foods biscuits, chocolates, sardines, packets of sweets, packets of cornflakes etc. Christina did not know what some of the tins and packets contained.

In the course of their conversation the boy asked them what they would like to eat. Christina had already seen the type of biscuits that Grace brought to school and pointed at it. The boy picked up a packet and gave her. They opened it and started eating. She could not believe her luck. A whole packet! The crunchiness and milky sweet taste that filled her mouth also filled her with expectancy for more.

Soon another boy entered the shop. Christina thought he was a customer, but was surprised when the two boys started speaking the Ibo language. Grace warned them to stop. She did not want her friend to become suspicious. They stopped and turned to pidgin but did continue what they were saying. They again engaged the girls in conversation asking them how they were preparing for the youth day. The conversation soon turned to the type of business they were carrying out and the large sums of money they used in buying the goods that were sold in the shop. Christina never believed that a single person could own such large sums of money. Then she remembered the piles of money she had seen in front of the woman who owned the shop in their neighbourhood. The ease, with which these boys spoke about money and the variety of goods in the shop, convinced her that these boys were indeed rich.

Soon the other boy invited the two girls to come over to his own shop. Ha sold ladies' dresses, under wears ,waist sleeves, breast wears and towels. These two boys were workers for two Ibo men who were their masters and the real owners of the shops, but they posed as the owners of the shops. As they talked, Grace exclaimed.

'I have forgotten my bag in Paul's shop. Let me go and take it. I will not be long' she went out of the shop leaving Christina behind. Bernard who was left with Christiana picked up two under wears and asked her if she liked them. She was excited at the offer and accepted them. He wrapped them up and gave her. After this he came and sat near her and put his arm round her. Christina moved away embarrassed.

'Why are you moving away?' the boy asked.' I don't bite' He moved nearer her again and put his arms round her. Again she moved away.

'Don't be a baby' Bernard chided her. 'Okay, come let me show you something' he said and led the way to a curtained – off section. Being called a baby had reminded her of the day Pascaline and her friends had called her a baby. She wanted to prove to herself that she was no longer a baby. She was a big girl now in secondary school. She followed Bernard into a small room at the back of the shop. As soon as she stepped in, the boy sent his arms round her and held her close. He tried to bring his mouth near to hers but she turned her face away protesting.

'Bernard, I do not like what you are doing.'

'What am I doing? I am just holding you'

Please let me go'

He promised her a dress, money, anything she wanted, if only she did not refuse him. Christina could not believe that this was happening to her. AS she struggled with Bernard, she prayed that Grace should come back quickly. Christina could not understand why her body was reacting the way it did. She liked the way the boy held her and spoke to her though she was scared. When he pulled off her under wear Christina realized his intentions and struggled harder. But Bernard was stronger than her. He pushed her on the make-shift bed on the floor and held her down. She wanted to scream but was afraid of alerting those in the nearby shops

She had looked forward to discovering the mystery in what the girls had been saying about boyfriends, but she never thought it would be this way. As soon as she felt a sharp pain she stifled a scream and tried to get up. But Bernard had not finished with her. Christina sank her nails on the flesh at the back of his neck. He released her and she got up quickly and started putting on her under wear. Then she saw the blood. Bernard himself was surprised at her reaction. When he realised what was happening he got a packet of sanitary pads and gave her. Before she left the shop, he stuffed a thousand francs into her palm.

The mystery was broken in such an unexpected manner that Christina was confused. She had not expected it to be so scaring and painful. She hardly knew the boy. She wanted to know what lay behind all what the girls been saying. Now she knew but did not really know.

Christina did not wait for Grace. As she walked home she felt sore between her legs. She felt unhappy and depressed. It had all been so disappointing. She sent her hand into her pocket and felt the money. It did not cheer her up. She now realised that this was how Grace got all the money, biscuits, sweets and chocolate that she brought to school. With this realization she wondered where Grace was.

Back home Christina took the broken mirror into her room and looked at her body. She looked at her breast. She touched them. They were swollen and tender to the touch. She looked at her Venus mound to find out if anything had changed, then she looked at her face. Nothing had changed, but everything had changed. That month Christina did not see the flow of blood.

An Event In Professor Abanu's Life

Professor Abanu had no real problem with anyone in his department. As head of the History Department in the University of Buea , he cherished a cordial relationship with his colleagues and auxiliary staff and even loved the idea of a father figure amongst his colleagues and even with the students. As a British trained scholar of the seventies he still held fast to the values and ideals of his era. He was meticulous about how he dressed to come to school. He believed that a scholarly person should dress scholarly, that is to say in a suit or at least a long sleeved shirt and a tie. The new-fangled way where men wore shirts and coats without a tie or a coat over a tee shirt grated on his sense of propriety.

The female students and some female staff did not conform to his idea of decency in dressing. When the Vice Chancellor passed a law on dressing etiquette on campus, Professor Abanu was relieved. He welcomed the idea and looked forward to not seeing girls' thighs and breasts through transparent blouses. But this was short-lived and the situation went back to its previous state. Professor Abanu was disappointed.

What made Professor Abanu most uncomfortable as the academic dishonesty that came as the result of the relationship between female students and lecturers, what the VC once called sexually transmitted marks. For the eight years that Professor Abanu had been at the university he was gradually accommodating these deficiencies much against his will, but there was this lecturer named Yateh in his department whom he could not bring himself to like in spite of the father figure he had created for himself. Yateh had a doctorate degree in history and was one of the promising lecturers in this department. He devoted so much to his work and was already preparing his first treatise for publication which would give him the rank of senior lecturer. He loved his job and found the requirements for growth challenging. Professor Abanu admired this in him. He was a doctor and deserved to be addressed as such but he was called Yateh by both staff and students. He did not mind it but Professor Abanu found this a bit unconventional and wondered how this had come to be. Having a doctorate degree was not easy and if anyone had it he deserved the honour to be addressed as such. But Yateh was different. He was at ease everywhere among his colleagues as well as among students. His affability did not lose him respect from the students. He was the type of modern teacher who identified with his students without losing their respect. Professor Abanu could not understand this.

Yateh was flashy, so flashy that even the way he walked seemed to be an affectation. It was even said that he had affairs with some of his female students. Professor Abanu as a rule did not give credit to such rumours but in Yates's case he was ready to make an exception. One day after working late into the afternoon, as he was locking his door to go home, he saw a pretty first year girl leaving Yateh's office in tears. Students at times cry over poor grades, but this girl's misery was caused by something else. It looked more like the result of a broken heart than a C minus.

Professor Abanu and Yateh belong to the same parish and went to the same Catholic Church in Molyko. Professor Abanu who liked to sit at the back of the church usually saw Yateh with his wife and two children, a boy and a girl, come in and sit at the front of the church. Each time they came to church he could see Yateh's influence on them. The wife was always dressed in bright coloured lace wrappers and blouse and the canopy shaped headgear of the Ibo and Yoruba women. The girl wore heavy plaits on her head with many brightly coloured beads attached to them. He usually wondered whether the plaits and beads were not too heavy for the child. The little boy wore brightly coloured jumpers made from cloth or lace materials like that of the mother.

Seeing Yateh with his family and how he would carry the little girl as she slept made Professor Abanu to feel kindly towards him. Then Yateh would turn to look at his wife, or at other members of the congregation and the gold chain on his neck would flash and professor Abanu would hate him again. The Sunday after he had seen the girl leave Yateh's office, Professor Abanu had watched him go up for communion, then came back to keel with bowed head and closed eyes. Was he praying for forgiveness for what he had done or he was reciting the prescribed prayers after communion? Professor Abanu wondered. He also wondered where Yateh found the time to do the things he did in addition to his heavy work load. He always met his deadlines with the student's scripts as well as with the completion of his course work. Where did he find the time to spend romancing girls who were still to understand why they were in the university, who were still experimenting with their relationship with men as well as trying on new shades of lipstick and perfumes? Did Mrs. Yateh know what her husband was doing? These thoughts went through Professor Abanu's mind as the mass ended and the announcements were being read.

Professor Abanu raised these problems with his wife that evening. Both of them were ardent Catholic Christians and

Mrs Abanu was the president of the women's group in the parish. They often talked about other people's weaknesses and infidelities. This was not to judge or condemn them, for; whatever they said did not affect those concerned. They did this as a means of reassuring themselves that they were making an effort at maintaining a close relationship with each other and with God by obeying the Ten Commandments.

In response to what her husband had told her about Yateh, she had said that there were many reasons for which a girl would leave a lecturers office in tears. Girls were emotionally charged and a little rudeness, rebuke or even a misunderstanding can set off the water works. She advised her husband not to make any conclusions on the situation until he knew more. He was impressed by his wife insightful assessment of the situation and pretended to agree with her.

In May the midyear Faculty Meeting had taken place at the university campus and many controversies had arisen concerning the revision of the undergraduate course work to be a continuum from the Advanced Level coursework. An the end another meeting had been scheduled to take place three months later during which teachers of history in secondary schools will be invited as they were an integral part of the teaching/ learning process that prepared students for the university. They had to be involved in the decisions affecting the content of the courses for a balanced and effective continuation. The meeting was scheduled to take place in Limbe at the conference hall of the Limbe Seaside Hotel. From what had happened at the faculty meeting, Professor Abanu knew that there was a real danger of the meeting ending in a deadlock. The university lecturers did not see amongst themselves. The situation was going to be worse with the presence of the secondary school teachers with their own ideas. He thought he had to be present to be an eye witness of what was going to happen. He did not want to hear it second hand. As head of department he had to be there, but he was fed up with some of the unrealistic suggestions that had been made during the previous meetings and the egocentric attitudes that had been displayed. He had wondered why scholars like his colleagues did not stick to the essentials that were academic, they had to bring in issues that had nothing to do with academics.

The meeting was scheduled to begin at eight a.m. on a Saturday morning. That Friday evening Professor Abanu had a call from Yateh. Dr. Yateh was scheduled to present the first paper for discussions. The battery of his car had gone down and it would take at least five hours for it to be recharged and he did not know where he could get another battery. The only person he could think of who was going to Limbe for the meeting was Professor Abanu. He asked if he would be kind enough to give him a lift to Limbe. After agreeing to pick him up he hung up the phone and complained to his wife.

'Dammit! Imagine who should call me asking for a ride to Limbe'

'Who'

'Yateh. Does he think that after openly opposing my ideas during the last faculty meeting, I am going to gladly carry him to Limbe?'

'What did you tell him?'

'There was no way I could refuse from the way he asked for help. Moreover I could not think of any tangible reason to give him for I am surely going to meet him at the meeting.'

'Good', Mrs. Abanu replied.

'Why do you say that?'

'You are the head of department and should not allow yourself to be mean over events dealing with your subordinates.'

Professor Abanu picked Yateh up at the entrance to the university and they drove off. As Professor Abanu had expected Yateh was dressed in one of his flamboyant outfits that so much unnerved him. He had put on a colourful jumper and matching trousers. To professor Abanu this was an academic meeting and he had to dress accordingly in a suit. This was not a traditional occasion. He kept his musings to himself as Yateh sat by him in the front passenger seat.

In spite of his colourfully outfit Yateh looked taciturn and preoccupied. Professor Abanu thought he was having second thoughts on their recent quarrel and was feeling bad because he in turn was being so kind to him to give him a lift to Limbe. As they drove from mile seventeen to Mutengene, Yateh tried calling someone on his cell phone. He frowned and fiddled with his phone complaining about the poor network. When they got down to Mutengene he asked Professor Abanu to pull over at a phone booth so that he could make a call. The booth was an open attachment outside a documentation kiosk. Professor Abanu watched him in the booth frowning and gesticulating like an actor on stage. When Yateh got back to the car he wore an expression of torment and anger. Professor Abanu felt obliged to ask what was wrong.

'What's going on, you look so... I do not know whether to say angry or frustrated.'

'That guy is trying to mess me up' Then Yateh realised that he was not sure of how Professor Abanu was going to receive what he was going to say. He continued with an elusive tone.

40

'It is something that might not interest you' then he thought he should tell him to get his reaction, after all it might interest him since they were in the same department.

'I have written this textbook on Advanced Level History and expected the printers to supply it this past week but till today I have got no response from them. Now they are telling me that they can only bring them at the end of the month.

Professor Abanu sat quiet for some time. He wondered whether Yateh was conscious of what he had just done. He looked at his profile to see if the realisation had dawn on him, but Yateh sat as if he had said nothing extra ordinary.

Professor Abanu had thought that the call was in connection to the girl who had left Yateh's office in tears. Maybe she was pregnant and Yateh did not want to accept responsibility for the pregnancy. This trend of thought had been to fuel his dislike for Yateh, but his mention of what he had done brought back memories of what had happened during the faculty meeting. While Professor Abanu battled with deciding which story to believe, for he wanted to believe in his speculation on the pregnant girl, his wife's words came back to him. He decided to take a neutral course because his natural response to what Yateh had told him or what he had thought was going on was not going to be pleasant. In a nonchalant voice he said 'Let me know if there is anything I can do to help'

'That's so nice of you. Thank you. You know I have always looked on you as a father. I don't know why, but I always have this feeling when I am with you'

Professor Abanu immediately felt elated. He loved it when people acknowledged him thus. His elation vanished when he turned to look at Yateh. Yateh was looking straight through the windscreen of the car and fiddling with the gold

41

chain on his neck. He was smiling too. He had on what Professor Abanu had come to describe as a roguish smile. He had seen this smile many times on the faces of his students and colleagues. The circumstances under which these smiles had been produced were indicative of the insincerity of the smiles. This usually drove him crazy, as he knew that they were not being sincere yet there was nothing he could do about it. Yateh continued.

'Have you ever been disappointed?'

'Disappointed?'

'Yes disappointed'

'What do you mean?

'I mean just disappointed. Dislike and irritation was building up into anger. Professor Abanu looked at Yateh and wondered why he had accepted to give him a lift to Limbe. The young man just rubbed him the wrong way though he had nothing tangible against him.

'Forget it'. Yateh said after sometime and laughed. Nothing again was said between them.

Professor Abanu finally reasoned away his dislike for Yateh pinning it on generation crisis, but the question worried him. Had he ever been disappointed? Yes many times but to pick out one that really hurt was not easy.

As the tyres of the car rolled on the tarmac producing a somnolent sound and vibration, Professor Abanu's mind went back to the past. 'Have I ever been disappointed?' He asked himself. Yes and it had really hurt

The first time had been when he had written the Advanced Levels. In upper sixth he had been earmarked as a grade A student in History. His capacity for remembering dates, persons and events had been enormous. His classmates always came to him for assistance. This had made him proud of himself though he had always been of help to his friends. His over confidence had been his undoing. He himself did not understand what had happened during marking. The results came out and he had the second to the last grade, a grade D. Although he had passed in three papers with good grades in the other two subjects he was very disappointed. When his parents friends and teachers had asked him what had happened he could not give any answer. While at the university he had written history again just to prove to himself that he could do it. Though he had an A grade, it was not the same. The harm had been done.

The second had to do with a girl when he was in the second year at the university. He had heard of how boys lost their heads over girls and eventually spent more than three years to get their first degree. He was determined to get his degree in three years. During his first year he had ignored the girls, but there was this girl who lived next door to him. She was so nice and kind and considerate. She too believed in making her degree in three years. They had much in common and felt at ease in each other's company. After the second semester of the second year, he had thought that he was matured enough to handle girls without being carried away. He was getting to the age of thinking about getting married. He was not interested in just getting a girlfriend. He wanted a lasting relationship, but he had to begin with this. He liked Bernadette the girl next door. He liked the way she looked at life. To him she looked a suitable girl and decided to go a step further. He had to get Bernadette to start looking at him differently. He had to work hard to archive this. Because they were so close he could discuss anything with her. They often ate together, but the first time he had patted her buttocks she had looked at him with a strange expression on her face. This had deterred him.

One evening he had declared his love for her and it had sounded so strange to her. He had thought that she could have seen it coming through his actions and endearing words. In an almost mother-like and condescending voice she had told him that she had a fiancé. He had been devastated but pretended that he did not mind. Until he left university, he never thought again of getting close, especially emotionally close to any girl. He had to change his apartment because he could not bear seeing her every day.

The meeting was not a success. One of the members of the Association of History teachers in the South West Province was notorious for coming out with polycopies of pirated notes from textbooks, which he insisted that his students must buy. There had been much opposition to this and the general feeling was that students should be encouraged to buy these polycopies not forced. The buying of the polycopies should not be used as a condition for passing a test or end of year examinations. The university lecturers had been vehemently against this practice but recently news had been moving along the grapevine that a university lecturer was also involved in the production of polycopies. Professor Abanu wondered whether this suspected lecturer was Yateh. If so then this was not his first production of polycopies. If this was the case then he now had something to throw in his face in the next faculty meeting.

More coal was added to the flames over the issue of the amalgamation of the history syllabuses. In the advent of this amalgamation Yateh had been fast. His intuition had been well timed and he had worked on a textbook containing the new proposed syllabus. It was not to be in a polycopy form but in a book form, but this was not the time to reveal the ace he had up his sleeve. During coffee break, the culprit teacher, believing that his ideas and intentions did him credit, persistently dragged anyone with a willing ear into a conversation to sound out what they thought about his ideas.

As they held their coffee mugs and milled around Professor Abanu saw a woman who had come in during the discussions. She was talking with the teacher with the polycopies. Professor Abanu looked at the teacher who was smirking to himself and hoped that the young man was not the type of academic who believed that his ideas were not accepted because they were too profound or original. He walked over to them. He had heard about the young man but had never met him. This was his opportunity.

'Good morning, nice coffee eh? Good to have young men with such ideas.' The young man's ideas had not received any approval and professor Abanu was amongst those who came out clear against them. He continued. 'Tell me, what are you working on now?'

The young man put down his mug and walked past Professor Abanu out of the room.

'That was unfortunate' the woman said. Professor Abanu turned and looked at her. She was striking, not really beautiful but very dark with lush natural hair pulled into a pony tail behind her head. 'Have a piece of cake' she offered. Professor Abanu looked at the plate and shook his head.

'I do not want to increase my waistline.' The woman lowered the plate as if she had been slapped in the face. She had done the catering and had come out to make sure that her guests were enjoying the food. Professor Abanu felt bad and gripped her hand as she turned away.

'You prepared all these, didn't you? He asked indicating the area where the snacks had been kept on a table. 'I am sorry I said that, I thought I was being clever'

'It's alright' she replied

'I am going to keep my mouth shut from now on. Every time I open it I hurt some one's feeling.

'I am not hurt,' the woman answered. 'In my profession, I meet lots of people and try to accommodate their differences. It is quite interesting to meet people. I get to know so much just by listening to my customer's conversations.' She leaned towards Professor Abanu and spoke quietly as if imparting confidences. Her lips were full and like the wife of Bath she had gap tooth. Professor Abanu who had done literature in high school was about to tell her that in Chaucer's time it was believed that a gap toothed woman was sensual, but decided not to. She might take it wrong.

'You are a good cook' he praised her'

'Yes, I learnt to cook at school'

Professor Abanu was impressed. He had never really given thought to the subjects taught in technical schools and believed that those who went to technical schools were those who were incapable of coping with general education subjects. He wanted to conversation to end there but the women continued to ask him question and he felt he had to ask her some questions as well. From her responses to his questions he got to know that she had gone to the University of Ngaoundere where she had done Food and Nutrition and Catering.

The discussions in the hall resumed at eleven a.m. and continued till lunch time. After lunch the members went into workshops to come out with suggestions and resolutions. Professor Abanu, Yateh and the teacher with the policopies

46

found themselves in the same workshop group. Theirs was a series of heated arguments. After the workshop session the various suggestions and resolutions were read out and either approved of or discarded with. Three participants were selected to organize the material, put it in booklet form, produce more copies and distribute them according to the institutions. It was seven p.m. before the meeting was declared closed.

It was raining outside. The bright lights and the heated arguments inside the conference room had made the participants oblivious to what was going on outside. The meeting was over and members were drifting outside. Some were reluctant to do so because they did not have cars of their own and had to depend on others for a lift or wait for the rain to stop for them to move to the roadside and get a taxi. Even those who had cars had to wait for the heavy down pour to abate before they could dash to their cars.

Professor Abanu was not pleased with some of the resolutions that had been adopted. He was standing at the veranda trying not to think about it. The polycopy teacher was again talking to another man trying to explain what he had meant when he had said that history was a subject that needed to move with the times. His suggestion had been so outrageous that when nobody had responded to it Professor Abanu had taken upon himself to set him right. It seemed as if he was talking with the intention of letting Professor Abanu to hear what he was saying, but Professor Abanu moved away to the other side of the veranda where Yateh was standing. In the semi darkness of that area he had not noticed that he was the one. It seemed as if God was putting him to the test. As the two people he wanted to avoid were now so near to him

47

and moving away would make him look rude and mean. He did not want to appear as running away, so he stayed put.

'You really went after him, sir.' Yateh observed as he came to stand by him

'I did not intend to go after anyone' Professor Abanu was not in the mood for conversation especially with Yateh. He had the impression that Yateh was leading to ask for a ride back to Buea. He had brought him down but they had not talked about going back. He did not want Yateh to take advantage of him. To bring the conversation to an end, Professor Abanu continued. 'He was speaking from his point of view and I was speaking from mine. That is what we were supposed to be doing, weren't we?'

'You mean that you were speaking from the right point of view and he from the wrong point of view?

'I think so, what do you think?'

'He is just a young man with young ideas.'

'And I am just an old man with old ideas, but mark you these old ideas have stood the test of time.'

'I envy you, sir, you are always so sure of yourself'

At that moment one of the teachers who had been selected to compile the resolutions came out of the hall and called Professor Abanu back into the hall. As he went he hoped that Yateh was not going to wait for him.

When he came out a few minutes later, Yateh had gone. In spite of all that he had done for the objective of the meeting to be archived, he felt awful and down cast. He was not in the mood to drive alone in the cold and rain back to Buea. It was a Saturday and Professor Abanu wanted something to cheer him up before he went home. He immediately decided on the Bota Senior Service Club.

As he slowed down at the entrance of the Seaside Hotel, waiting for other vehicles to pass before he got into the highway, he saw the lady with whom he had spoken during the coffee break. He stopped and wound down his window. When she noticed that he was the one, she folded her umbrella and got into the car.

'Hm, what a wet evening.' She observed.

'And a nasty day' Professor Abanu corroborated.

'Why do you say that?' she asked. Professor Abanu turned and looked at her. She had told him that her name was Susanna. It was such an old fashioned and comfortable name. He had a feeling in his gut that the name reflected the person. His mind was straying.

'I am just weary. Where should I drop you?'

'In fact, I am going home. I live in GRA'. Then she went back to the topic professor Abanu had dropped.' You said you are weary. Weariness is tiredness of the spirit not the body'

'How poetic' he replied. 'You should have done literature not catering'

'In fact I love literature. I love reading'

To hear this from a woman who spent her time cooking was something. He wanted to get to know her.

'I am going to the SS Club in Bota. Why don't you come along?'

It was said before he realized the enormity of what he had done, but his anxiety was short-lived when they arrived at the club. There was a party going on and parking was a problem. He dropped Susanna before manoeuvring into an empty space a distance away from the main building of the club. By the time he got into the club, Susanna was already chatting with a group of men. She was a member of the club but professor Abanu did not know this. Since they did not come in together they would not be linked to each other. Professor Abanu was grateful for this but he could not completely ignore her. He walked up to the group. He knew two of the men. The third he did not. Before he could say anything Susanna said.

'Please, meet Professor Abanu. He rescued me from the rain.' Pleasantries were exchanged and the professor was soon seated with her, but the atmosphere did not permit any serious conversation.

They seeped on their beers and watched couples dancing. Susanna was used to mixing with people during social events and could not just sit down and watch. She invited him for a dance. He could not resist. He wanted to get this heaviness out of his system. He was not a good dancer but danced out of politeness. Susanna encouraged him and he was soon enjoying watching her dance with him. Later on Professor Abanu was standing at the counter when he turned round and saw Yateh. He did not know when he had come in. Maybe he had seen him dancing with Susanna. He had only realized that he had been holding her passionately when she whispered in his ears 'I love that but watch out.' May be Yateh had seen this.

Professor Abanu was enjoying himself. The tension in him was easing off. His mental as well as physical muscles were relaxing. He felt happy. He wanted to believe what the musicians were saying, that the world was beautiful and people were good. Man was made to be happy, and we would be more beautiful and happy when we let ourselves go, when we shouted when we wanted to shout, ran about naked like little kids when we wanted to and embrace each other when we wanted to. The beer and atmosphere were making all these possible.

It was midnight before professor Abanu realised how late it was. He was in a fix. He had not planned to spend the night in Limbe. He hadn't enough money to pay a hotel room. He was too tipsy to drive back to Buea that night. The risks too were enormous considering the fact that he had to drive through Mutengene notorious for its rough night life.

When he left the Bata Senior Service Club he was happy that Susanna was with him. He had not made any statement about where he was going to spend the night because he himself did not know. He had friends and family members in Limbe but he thought it was not good for him to go to then at that time of the night. It was not a responsible action and he was a responsible man. He could not equally suggest anything to Susanna. A man is always a man and he was going to find a way out of this even if it meant driving back to Buea.

As they drove to GRA Susanna believed that her partner was going to drive back to Buea after dropping her and she was concerned. When they arrived at her door he had made up his mind to drive back to Buea, but Susanna surprised him by inviting him to spend the night.

'It would be ungrateful of me to allow you to drive back to Buea at this time of the night. If anything happens to you I will never be able to live with my conscience.. I have a guest room, no strings attached' Professor Abanu did not reply to this. He just followed her into the house and into the guest room. When he closed the door he sank on the bed and passed out.

At five thirty the next morning Professor Abanu was on his way back to Buea. He was always an early riser. Sitting beside him was Susanna. She had decided to use this opportunity to visit her sister who lived in Buea. She decided to leave so early because she intended to come back by midday because she had some work to do in preparation for Monday.

As they ascended the Plantecam Hill after Mutengene, a group of passengers were standing beside a taxi. The taxi's bonnet was open and the driver was fidgeting with the engine. As he approached he saw somebody waving him down. He slowed. It was Yateh. He stopped. Professor Abanu saw his gaze go past him to his passenger. The Yateh said as he got into the car. 'We came down together and God want us to go back together' Professor Abanu did not respond to this. He had not expected this to happen. Susanna's presence said it all. When he thought about what he had done in the early hours of the morning he felt heartsick and blamed the beer he had drank, but underneath all there was a little thrill.

Professor Abanu said very little on the way home. Yateh spoke about some of the issues that had been raised at the meeting. He was behaving as if they had just left the meeting and was discussing about it. Susanna said nothing. Their silence intrigued Yateh. Then the implication of the situation dawned on him. He was at once surprised and more intrigued.

They dropped Susanna at Unisport and continued up the street. Yateh could not help probing a little further

'You must have had a very pleasant night, but don't worry. I never saw you with anybody.' They had arrived at Yateh's entrance and Professor Abanu thought that he should clear the air.

'It was not like you think'

'It never is' Yateh replied as he got out of the car. 'Thank you very much. It was hectic at the SS club last night. See you in school tomorrow prof.'

Professor Abanu decided not to tell his wife. He had spent nights out impromptu after meetings with colleagues and sometimes after family meetings. This was going to be just one of such nights. His wife trusted him and he was pleased to be the man she thought he was, but now he was different. He thought he had no right to do this to her. He would have to pretend as if nothing had happened. He owed her that. A chapter of his life was closing and another was opening. He wanted to capture this moment with the right sentiment

Never again would he sit at the back of the church and watch Yateh. From now hence he would sit in front and let Yateh, knowing what he knew watch him. He would have to mentally knell before Yateh, as we must all do, kneel before one another and before the one who is above us all.

Though this chapter of his life was closing and another opening it was not for him alone. He kept receiving phone calls from Susanna. Mrs Abanu while sorting out his clothes to be washed had smelled a strange perfume on his shirt. Then she went through the rest of his clothes and smelt the same distinctive perfume. There had to be an explanation for this.

No matter how long she sat on the bed and wondered as she held her head in her hands, she could not imagine any answer. Yet her husband was such a warm and loving husband that she felt unreasonable with her fears and doubts. Yet the doubts passed from her mind to her body. It periodically became one of those momentary flutters that stops you cold from time to time and only goes away with the passage of time.

Next-Door Neighbours

'Mummy! Mummy! Some people came into that compound yesterday'
'Which compound?'
The compound next to ours'
'What did they do?'
'One man opened the door and they went inside. Then they came outside and looked round the house and went away'
'Maybe we will soon have neighbours. The darkness in the compound at night frightens me'
'YEAH. Yeah!' Junior shouted 'I will soon have friends to play with apart from Small Mami'
'How do you know that the family coming to live in that house will have children?'
'They should have. Every family should have children'
'Some do not' the mother replied.
'Why'? Junior asked
'Well... Well, it just happens.'
'Why does it just happen?' Junior persisted
'Some don't want to and God does not give to others'
'Why is God so cruel? Every family should have children. When Small Mami was born Grandma said children are a blessing from God. Why does he not bless some families?'
'Junior! Junior!'
'Yes Daddy!' Junior ran out of the kitchen to meet his father in the bedroom. Small mami was sitting on her chamber pot in the bathroom and did not want to be left alone. The toilet roll was finished and her father could not leave her alone to get another from the cupboard, so he had

to call for junior to keep her company. Left in the kitchen Mrs. Ngong contemplated the question her five year old son had asked her. It was too early in the morning to start having such serious thoughts. She liked the idea that they were going to have neighbours. Three days later people came to the house next door and started cleaning up both inside and outside. The house had been unoccupied for almost a year. The lawn was overgrown and weeds had overtaken the garden space behind the house. There were cobwebs on the eaves and the walls needed a coat of paint. The cemented yard was covered with moss.

Only a certain class of people live in Foncha Street in Bamenda. When Mr. Cletus Ngong was transferred from Douala to Bamenda, he had asked a friend to look for a hoist for him. When he came up to Bamenda and saw the house he was very pleased. In Douala he had to make do with what he could get, but in Bamenda his friend had many choices. And his choice was good.

Mr. Ngong's family had moved into the second house on a line of houses on one of the side streets leading off the main Foncha Street. He was happy that at last he was living in a neighbourhood that fitted his status. This was his third year of living in the house and he was pleased with it. Though the rents were high it was not up to what he had paid in Douala for a house that did not have half of the facilities that this one had.

Two nights after the cleaning of the house next door, Mr. Cletus Ngong was awaken from sleep by the noise of a truck reversing and the voices of people. He had no idea of what was happening. His dog was barking furiously so he got up and went into the bathroom whose window was facing the side of the house next door. He saw what was happening and went back to bed. His wife Judith was awake already.

'What is happening outside?' she asked

'It seems as if we have new neighbours'

'Oh, so they have come'

'Do you know them/'

'No, but Junior told me last week that the compound was being cleaned. We will know in the morning. Let's go to sleep'

But they could not sleep. Judith was hoping that the women coming to live next door would be friendly. She like friendly neighbours. Her former neighbour in the other building on the left of their house, Mrs. Che Mba had been a proud and haughty woman. She had tried to be friendly with her. In her effort at being friends with her it had looked as if she was begging for her friendship. But Mr. Ngong and Mr. Che Mba had hit it off as soon as they had met. They were both ex-students of Sacred Heart College Mankon. They always seemed to be vibrating on the same wavelength. Some Shesa Alumni vibes kept them together. The men soon realized that the evening visits they enjoyed together were a strain on the women and decided to stop it and meet in Club 58 instead. It was a public place where the women were not obliges to talk to each other. It was also not often that the men took their wives there on the same evening. Mr. Ngong thought of hid friend Mr. Che Mba for a while before he fell asleep. Being a top civil servant was not easy on the family. Hardly are you settled in a town you are again transferred to another. Mr. Che Mba had made just four years in Bamenda before he was transferred back to Yaounde from where he had come to Bamenda.

Two days passed without Mr. Ngong and his wife seeing their new neighbours, But Junior had heard the voices of children in the house and had gone one evening and waited near the back fence to see them. His ten minutes of waiting was rewarded when two boys dashed out of the kitchen. The first was about seven years old and the second was Junior's age. He looked at them but they did not see him as they dashed back into the house.

Mrs. Ngong was dying to meet the new women but did not want to appear too anxious. Her experience with Mrs. Che Mba had taught her a lesson. It was the Month of August and a week before schools reopened. In the frenzy of preparing the children to go back to school Mr. Ngong had forgotten about the new neighbours. Junior was going into class one in the primary section and Small mami was going into Nursery One. The family had one car and it was Mr. Ngong's duty to take the children to school and bring them back. On days he was not able to do so, the house help would take them to school and go for them after school.

Mr. Ngong was the manager of the Bank for Internal and External Investment, B.I.E.I, located along Commercial Avenue in Bamenda. He was the boss and could not be controlled by anybody. He was satisfied with his job and his family life.

It was a Monday, one week after schools reopened and Mr. Ngong was reversing out of his garage unto the side street that led to the main street. Junior and Small Mami were sitting behind. Mr. Yango, the man whose family had moved in next door was also reversing out of his garage unto the same side street. The two cars were parallel. Junior saw the children sitting behind their father's car.

'Daddy, the children next door come to our school'

Mr. Ngong looked at the other car. It was a Land Cruiser. He stopped to look at the man driving the car. Mr. Yango concentrated on his manoeuvre out of the garage and drove off. Mr. Ngong held his breath. He could not believe his eyes. That bastard! He cursed under his breath. Memories of that campaign period in C.C.A.S.T Bambili came back to him as if it was yesterday. He had never been so angry and humiliated in his life.

Campaigns for officials to handle the student union for the next academic year had been lunched. Some staff members and some of his friends had encouraged him to stand for the Students Union President. He Cletus Ngong was a legible candidate as he fulfilled the conditions the administration had put one of which was academic excellence. He had accepted and the two other boys who were to stand with him were equally good but he had taken the prize for the student with the highest annual average in both the arts and the sciences. So he had an edge over them. The conditions for candidature were again read out during morning assembly on the Monday of Campaign week. Things were moving smoothly as the three boys came up with various manoeuvres and strategies to win more students to their side. They had five days to do their campaigns. Elections were to take place on Saturday. It was already Friday and fliers had been pasted at strategic locations on campus. The main notice board had carried some. The cypress trees on the way to the refectory were white with fliers of the three contenders. The walls and doors of the classrooms were covered with campaign graffiti. Cletus Ngong had scheduled his last campaign exercise for Friday evening in the Social Centre immediately after supper. He was poised to win over sixty per cent of the student population because he realized that they appreciated his eloquence and understanding of student's problems. His promised solutions to them too were down to earth though he spiced them with some dreams that he knew where never to come true. The students swallowed them all and cheered in the euphoria of campaign week.

On Friday evening the refectory was unusually empty. This did not bother Cletus because he knew that the other candidates were busy planning for this final evening as he had done. Moreover he knew that students will always be there to listen to him speak, for he always pulled a crowd.

The tension was mounting and he could barely eat his food. He was sitting in the refectory with his henchmen putting the final touches on their strategy. They were arranging how he would be led into the hall as the president elect of the students Union, for they were sure that they were going to win.

Cletus Ngong was dressed in a dark suit which he had rushed off to town to borrow the day before. Six boys equally dressed in suits flanked him. When he entered the hall he noticed that the crowd was not as large as he had expected. This did not bother him as students usually trickled in and before the evening was over the hall was always full. Because of this each candidate had arranged to come in with his entourage but would speak last. Usually two speakers spoke before the main speaker. They usually exalted their president's ideas and praised what he was going to do for the student body. Cletus and his inner circle had carefully mapped out their plan in such a way during the five days of campaign they had something new to tell the students each day. On this last day they were going to use their trump card.

The first speaker was James Ateh. He was a lower sixth science student. He spoke about the meals given to students. Using his knowledge of Biology he spoke of the nutrients in the food they ate and how they affected them mentally and physically. He spoke of the number of calories a teenager needs per day to carry out his or her activities and that what was provided in the refectory was not enough to provide this calorie need. Some of what he said was new to arts students who cheered not what he was saying but the information he was giving out. He crowned it all by talking about the bananas that accompanied lunch especially on Sundays. They were sure that the administration did not know the effect it had on boys. When this was said the girls shouted and booed. Girls did not like eating bananas and whenever a girl gave her bananas to a boy, he usually told her to be ready to take care of the after effects. The boys believed that eating bananas increased their virility and libido.

With the increased number of high schools in Cameroon, the subvention government gave to C.C.A.S.T. Bambili had drastically reduced. James Ateh spoke of the suggestions their president was going to give to the administration to improve on the student's meals with the funds available. Edwin Bawe spoke of the state if the hostels, the academic situation and extracurricular activities. The shouting of the students who were present was pulling many more students to the hall. His last point was a very sensitive issue which touched on the discipline of the school. This concerned the ban that had been placed on Spots Bar. Being caught dancing in Spots Bar meant instant dismissal. To this Edwin Bawe said that as teenagers they had a lot of energy and dancing in Spots Bar was one of the ways of expending this energy. If the students were not allowed to go to Spots Bar this energy would be directed to other avenues that would be disastrous to the students. They will be tempted to dodge to town, which was a more serious crime than going to Spots Bar. To this there was a thunderous applause which ended with the chant supporters had made up to praise their president

'Which way? The clear way!'

'Which way? The brain way!'

'Who is our president?'

Cletus the brain!'

''Cletus the mediator!'

Cletus Ngong stood up and raised his hands to calm the students. The noise had attracted the bookworms who were more interested in their studies than who became student union president. The hall was now full. Each of the candidates had one hour of campaign. Cletus Ngong had twenty minutes left to give way to the next candidate who was Bernard Yango.

Cletus Ngong stood up and told the students that C.C.A.S.T. Bambili was one of the nurseries for future leaders in Cameroon. He thanked the administration for the opportunity given to the students to start having a feel of what leadership and citizenship means. It was just right and proper that they should start assuming these roles as patriotic citizens. In the act of voting they were exercising their inalienable rights. He was also grateful that so far no unpleasant situation had arisen. This showed the level of maturity of the candidates and hoped that this atmosphere was going to continue to the end of the elections. He assured them that by voting him they were making the right choice. The students applauded and were once more quieted down by Cletus waving his hands for silence. He waited for complete silence for his next words to have the desired effect.

A roar outside broke the silence. Some students were singing and approaching the hall

'Who is Cletus?'

'Cletus the ngong dog!'

'Cletus the liar!'

'Cletus the impostor!'

'Who is Bernard?'

'Bernard the yankee!'

Bernard the cash boy!'

'Bernard the president!'

The crowd busted into the hall chanting these abuses against Cletus and praising Bernard Yango their president. Cletus was shocked at what was going on. He had thought that the whole exercise was going to be carried out in a straight forward manner, but things were turning out differently.

Bernard had given his campaign managers money to get a group of boys to start a smear campaign against Cletus. These boys had been taken to the Bambili Squares on a drinking spree after which they were going to move round the campus discouraging the students from voting for Cletus. When more boys heard that Bernard was giving free drinks to anybody who would vote for him the crowd had increased. The opportunity to have a free drink was tempting. The large crowd that gathered at the squares assured the campaign managers that they had succeeded in their strategy. Their plan was that they would get to the hall as soon as Cletus finished his making his speech so that he too would hear the abuses before he got away. The boys after drinking sixty litres of palm wine and two crates of beer were definitely drunk before they started their procession to the Social centre.

Cletus's one hour was not yet over when they interrupted him. This interruption together with the abuses being rained down on their president infuriated his supporters. Even some of the students who had not made up their mind and those who were not convinced enough to vote for Cletus were not happy with what was happening. Cletus's supporters quickly concerted and came out with their own chant.

'Who is Yango?'

'Yango the thief!'

'Yango, the corrupter!'

'Yango the duller!'

Then they repeated their chant praising Cletus their president. The angry chanting turned into a brawl. Yango's supporters were too drunk to be a match for Cletus's supporters. As students threw blows at random and some tried to rush out, the casualties increased.

The Senior Discipline Master heard the noise from his house and thought it was the usual noise that had been going on since the campaign began. When two students knocked at his door panting he knew that something had gone wrong. Before he arrived at the Social Centre the student's had all disappeared leaving behind the wounded, Cletus and his four henchmen, and a few supporters off Bernard. At that moment Bernard Yango appeared at the scene looking composed and well dressed. He acted more like an observer than a participant. He pretended to be ignorant of what had happened. The Senior Discipline Master called them aside and asked them to come along with two of their campaign managers. Cletus's four campaign managers wanted to come along but the discipline master refused. Bernard had only one campaign manager who was sober enough to follow him. The rest had disappeared.

In the discipline Master's office the two candidates were asked to wait outside while the supporters went in one after the other to be interviewed on what had happened. In the room that was used as waiting room Bernard Yango sat on a bench but made sure that he did not look at Cletus. Bernard had not foreseen that his strategy would go out of control. He was not present at the scene so he did not know exactly what had happened. Cletus sat on a bench opposite Bernard and glared at him.

From the evidence given by both parties it was evident that Bernard's supporters were the cause of the trouble but the wounds that Cletus's supporters had inflicted on their opponents were serious. Many of them were receiving treatment for wounds and laceration at the school's infirmary which was still open because it also served the villagers who lived round the school campus. For these reasons the elections for Saturday were suspended indefinitely.

The week after the suspension of the elections was hell for both parties. Cletus and Bernard were constantly called to the principal's office where they were questioned again and again. In the dormitories the war went on. The discipline masters living on campus made surprise checks in the dormitories at night to make sure that there was peace and security.

Cletus's supporters began a smear campaign against Bernard. They said he had stolen the money which he had used in buying drinks for the boys who had caused the whole problem. When his girlfriend heard this she jilted him. This was the last straw. Bernard could stand it no longer. He challenged Cletus to an open fight. This was reported to the school authorities who promised Bernard instant dismissal if he carried out his threats.

At the end of that week the principal summoned an extra ordinary assembly of staff and students in the school auditorium. He told the students that leadership cannot be gotten through dubious means or through violence. Leadership is a call to serve the people. Two of the candidates for the position of student Union president had failed in these two respects. The third candidate was the student union president. There was a general murmur from the students. There was no applause even from the supporters of the third candidate. From that day till they wrote the Advanced Level Examination, left school and went their separate ways, Cletus and Bernard never spoken to each other. They had not as much as met. They never bothered to know what had become of the other. Now fate had brought them together as neighbours. All these events went through Cletus's head as he drove to work that morning. Mr. Yango was not anxious to know who his neighbours were. He was still very much the Bernard Yango of C.C.A.S.T. Bambili, proud, arrogant and distant. To Mr. Ngong ten years had elapsed and it was as if it was yesterday that it had happened

Mrs. Ngong thought that three weeks were too much for her to resist moving over to her neighbour's house to welcome her. One afternoon on her day off from school, after she had finished cooking she moved over to her neighbour's house. She rang the bell at the gate and waited. Mrs. Yango was in the bedroom when she heard the sound of the bell. She could not imagine who would be coming to her house at that time of the day. Since they had come to Bamenda, the only persons who had come to their house had been her husband's friends. Anybody who was her husband's friend should know that at this time of the day he would be at work. As she thought these thoughts she walked to window of the bedroom which faced the front of the house to see who had rung the bell. She saw the woman who lived next door standing there. She had seen her one morning as she took her children to the car as they left for school. At first she was irritated then intrigued to find out what she wanted. Before the house help would open the door to tell her that a woman was looking for her, she was already opening the door. She moved along the corridor into the sitting room and out unto the veranda. The house help was opening the gate for Mrs. Ngong to come in. As soon as she saw Mrs. Yango standing outside there was a bright smile on her face. She moved the few steps up to the veranda and held Mrs. Yango's hands.'

I just came to welcome you to our neighbourhood. I could have come earlier but I wanted you to settle down before I come. My name is Judith.'

Mrs. Yango was pleasantly surprised. She did not know how to react to this. She was not expecting this type of reception. She too smiled and held Mrs. Ngong's hands. She opened the door and they went into the sitting room.

'Please sit down.' She invited Judith. She did not know what to say but remembered that the woman had introduced herself.

'My name is Alice' then she sat looking at Judith. In the towns where she had lived with her husband she had never had such an experience. There was an awkward silence. Judith realised that things were not moving and the situation was becoming embarrassing, but when encouraged her was the smile on Alice's face.

'I am sorry if I have disturbed you from what you were doing. I just thought that I should come here and welcome you and get to know you since we are now neighbours. Let me leave you to your work. I will come again some other time.' She made to get up from her seat.

'No, no, do not go yet. I am sorry that I have behaved badly'

'Do not say that.' Judith interrupted her. 'I know it can be embarrassing when someone just walks into your house'

'You have not just walked in. You have come to visit which is a good thing. I am so happy that you have come to welcome me. I have never been treated this way in the towns where I have lived. I am so grateful. Please do not think that I do not appreciate your sign of friendship. I am really grateful.'

There was nothing more for her to say. Alice was thinking furiously of what to say, when Judith came in again.

'Thank you for being so nice. I should be going. We are neighbours and will be seeing each other soon again.'

'That is true.' Alice replied. 'Next time it will be my turn to come to your house.' The women laughed as Judith got up and moved to the door. Alice hurried passed her and opened the door for her. Judith walked out of the house and out of the gate without looking back. Since she did not hear the door of the house shutting she knew that Alice had not yet gone back into the house but was standing outside watching her.

Mrs. Yango was delighted that her neighbour had come to welcome her to the neighbourhood. She had thought that things were going to be as they were in Douala where her neighbours minded their business and never greeted anybody. She liked to friendly with her neighbours but her experiences had thought her a lesson. She had wanted to know the town better but there was nobody to show her round. What she found particularly interesting was the cost of food items. They were unbelievably cheap and she had the impression that she was paying more than she should have because whatever the women asked for the food item she was buying she gave the money without bargaining because it was far less than what she would have paid in Douala. With someone who knew the town things were going to be different and she would be able to save a bit more money. The two women had become friends during their first meeting.

It was playtime at the Ngi Vicy International Nursery and Primary School located along Sonac Street. The boys were playing football. It was really a child's version of the game as the two opposing groups kicked the ball at random up and down the yard. Mr. Ngong's son Junior and Paddy, Mr. Yango's son were in the same group. They played closed to each other and passed the ball between them until the other players complained. They enjoyed playing together at school but at home they were not allowed to play with the neighbour's children.

Mr. Che Mba Martin was in town. He hadn't time to visit his friend Mr. Cletus at home but he could see him in his office. He stopped at the BIFI Bank and saw his friend's car parked in the managers' parking space. He knew that he was in and went in to see him. As soon as he entered the office Mr. Ngong shouted

'He! Chems! When did you get to town?

'I got in yesterday and I am travelling back to Yaoundé this afternoon. I don' have much time I would have come to the house, so I decided to come to the office' As he spoke he pulled out the visitor's chair and sat on it.

'You did well. How are Madam and the kids? Mr. Ngong asked.

'They are doing fine. How is it moving here?'

'Just great. How are you coping in Yaoundé?'

'Just fine, just fine.' He looked at his watch. It was getting to midday. Why don't we go somewhere and have a bite, it is midday already.'

Since they were just going to a place in town they decided to go in Mr. Ngong's car leaving Mr. Che Mba's at the bank premises. They drove off without agreeing on where they should go. They had been together so much so that wherever one of them decided for them to go the other knew it was a good place. Mr. Ngong drove to the Club 58 Up station.

Both had been members of the club but now Mr. Che Mba was a country member. He still had the right to sit at the counter. They were eating fried chicken, which Club 58 is famous for, and pushing it down with seeps of Sartzenbrau. It was a few minutes after midday and many more people were coming to the club for a bite and a drink.

Two men came in as Mr. Ngong and Mr. Che Mba were chatting. One was Mr. Yango. He was not a member of the club but as a potential member he had been invited by a friend who was a member. Incidentally, Mr. Wainga who had invited Mr. Yango knew Mr. Che Mba. As soon as they came in Mr. Wainga saw Mr. Che Mba and moved over to greet him. Mr. Yango moved along to greet the men sitting at the counter. Since Mr. Ngong and Mr. Che Mba had their backs to the door, Mr. Yango did not know who were sitting there. He shook hands with Mr. Che Mba and turned to great the other man and came face to face with his enemy of C.C.A.S.T. Bambili. Ten years receded in their minds and the old enmity sparkled in their eyes, but they shook hands all the same. They were both surprised at the intensity of hatred they found in each other's eyes. At that moment, within themselves they acknowledged the fact that they were neighbours. Mr. Yango had seen Mr. Ngong but did not want to acknowledge the fact that he was his neighbour and to do what neighbours are expected to do.

The evening meal was over in the Ngong house hold. Mr. Ngong and his wife were sitting in the parlour watching TV. The children were in the bedroom with the house help. Mr. Ngong was telling his wife about Mr. Che Mba's visit to his office and the greetings he had sent her.

'That reminds me.' Mrs Ngong remarked. 'I met with our neighbour today. She is such a nice woman. She is not like Mrs. Che Mba. I went to her house and ...'

'Never go there again' her husband interrupted her. Judith was so surprised that she did not know what to say. She waited for her husband to explain himself, but he did not. So she asked

'Why?'

'I said don't go there again.'

'I would like to know why you do not want me to go there. It was not my fault that I could not be friends with Mrs. Che Mba. You yourself know that I tried. Because you are friends with Mr. Che Mba does not mean that I had to be friends with his wife. It was unfortunate'

In the silence that ensured Mrs. Ngong looked at her husband. There were lines of anger on his brow and his eyes were very deep. Judith continued.

'The expression on your face shows that there is something between you and that family. What is it Cletus?'

Mr. Ngong regretted his outburst. He just wanted to ignore the neighbours and wanted his family to do the same.

'It is nothing Judith. I don't know what came over me. Forget it' But Judith did not; she wondered why her husband had forbidden her from ever visiting the neighbours. She imagined all sorts of reasons but nothing was tangible because Cletus had never given her any reason to suspect him of any foul dealings. She was confused and did not know how to bring up the subject again to get to the root of the matter.

Mr. And Mrs. Yango were lying in bed. Early in their marriage they had agreed never to discuss important issues in the presence of the children or any persons who lived with them. Whatever had to be discussed must be done in the bedroom. If they had to disagree or quarrel, it was in the bedroom. Mrs. Yango had observed her husband's reaction when the boys had talked about playing with the Ngong children at school. The boys adored Junior's younger sister and wanted her to come and play with them at home. She had thought that the reaction might have been the result of a minor irritation at the fact that she had not yet conceived to give him a little girl. Whatever the case, she had to say what was on her mind.

'Mrs. Ngong, our neighbour came to visit us today. She is such a nice woman. I now have a friend to help me know the town better.'

Mr. Yango did not reply. He wanted his wife to talk herself out and forget. But she did not.

'Why are you so silent Ben? I know you. You are not happy with what I have said. I can see it on your face.

'Alice please, I don't want to talk about it.'

'Talk about what? Has having nice neighbours become such an unpleasant topic for conversation?'

'I say I do not want to talk about neighbours' He turned and pulled the sheets up to his chin and stared at the ceiling. Alice was puzzled, but she had learnt early in their marriage that when her husband responded like that it meant that the topic was closed. She looked at her husband's profile. She could see the lines of anger. She kept quiet. She could not understand why a simple subject like having neighbours to visit can be such an unpleasant topic.

It was a tedious day for Mr. Yango. The meeting with the directors from Yaounde was taking longer than he had expected. After a twenty minutes break at midday he had thought that he was going to sneak out and pick up his children from school or send someone to take them home. Before he realized it was getting to two o clock. He could not leave the meeting because the directors kept calling on him to comment on the various reports that were presented. He went out for a few minutes to call his wife on her cell phone. She was not in town. She and some of her colleagues had accompanied one of their colleagues who had lost the father to Bali. Mr. Yango had not yet installed a fixed phone in his house to be able to call the house help to pick the children from school. He panicked but there was no way he could leave the meeting. He was distracted as he thought of what might be happening to his children. He got what was being said in bits and pieces as his mind kept straying to his boys left alone at school.

Mr. Ngong himself was a bit late in picking up his children from school. While they waited for their parents, the children amused themselves by playing with the many play gadgets in the school playground. Luke the younger of the Yango boys was at one end of the seesaw and Small Mami was on the other end squealing with laughter as she moved gently up and down. Paddy, the elder son and junior were both sitting on one swing with their hands round each other and the other holding the cord of the swing at both ends. They were laughing as they tried to make the swing go faster.

Mr. Ngong watched them for some time before calling out for his children.

'Junior!' Junior turned and saw his father and jumped off the swing. Paddy remained sitting on the swing. Junior stopped half way towards his father and beckoned for Paddy to come along. Paddy continued to sit on the swing watching to see what was going to happen. He really wanted to go home but even in school they had been warned not to enter the car of anybody who was not the one to take them home. Small Mami, holding Luke's hand was already running towards the car. She opened the back door and got in pulling Luke after her. When Paddy did not jump down from the swing Junior went back to him held his hand and pulled him down to come along with him. His younger brother was already in the car so he had no choice.

Mr. Ngong was trapped. He did not know what to do. Paddy had his eyes fixed on Mr. Ngong's face. There was nothing Mr. Ngong could do but to carry the children home. He usually bought yogurt and biscuits for his children on their way back from school. When they got to the shop where they usually stopped to buy these things, Small Mami Shouted.

'Stop! Stop! As she usually did, when they got to the front of the shop. Carrying Bernard Yango's children home was enough. Buying them yogurt and biscuits was another issue altogether, but there was nothing he could do. As soon as the stopped at the shop his children got out taking their friends along. As they ate at the back of the car on their way home the children talked about what they were going to do that afternoon. Paddy talked about what he was going to do with Luke and Junior talked about what he was going to do with Small Mami, but he did not feel enthusiastic. He would have preferred to go and play with Paddy and Luke He wanted to ask his father if he could go and play with the two boys but changed his mind. Just such thoughts were going on in Small Mami's mind. With the innocence of children who had no idea of what was going on between their parents Small Mami asked

'Daddy, can Paddy and Luke come and play with us?' Four pairs of eyes looked eagerly at the back of his head for a positive response. Mr. Ngong was grateful that the children were behind him and could not see his face. Children have a way of disarming their parents on issues they thought they were in total control. He did not answer immediately. He knew that he would never allow his children to go into that compound. Ten years was just like yesterday. Without conviction he replied.

'If their daddy will allow them, then that will be fine.'

Mr. Yango could not get out of the room when his guests were still there. He prayed for them to get over the formalities of closing the meeting. When this was being prolonged he went close to the Charge' de Mission and whispered in his ears that he wanted to rush and find out if his children had been taken home from school. The meeting was officially over so he could go. He got into his car and drove off. He drove as if the faster he went he would put back the time. He arrived at the school compound. It was deserted. He put off his car engine and came out of the car. He walked down to the rickety gate and pushed it open. The nursery section was the building behind. He walked towards it but everywhere was quiet. He was bewildered. He did not know where the head mistress lived. He called his wife to find out if she was already at home. She was on her way back from Bali when the call came through. She shouted when she was told that nobody had picked up the children from school and they were not in the school compound. It was now three thirty and he did not know where his children were. His wife's shout increased the adrenaline flow in his stomach. He got into his car and drove home in a daze.

The house help came to open the gate for him. As soon as he got to where the girl was standing holding the gate for him to pass he stopped and asked

'Did you go to pick up the children from school?'

'No sir.' Mr. Yango's heart was actually thudding now and he felt a pain in his chest. 'They are behind the house' the girl continued when she saw the pain in her master's face. Mr. Yango drove slowly into the garage and stopped the car. He sat for some time for his heart beat to slow down.. He got out of the car and instead of going into the house he walked by the side of the house to the backyard. Paddy and Luke were standing at the fence separating the two compounds. When they saw him they rushed towards him shouting.

'Daddy! Daddy! Junior's father brought us home today. He bought us Yogurt and biscuits'

Mr. Yango stooped to embrace his two sons, holding them close to his chest with his head between theirs. When he looked up he saw two pairs of eyes looking at him from between the railings of the fence. When Junior and Small Mami saw him looking at them they ran away.

Mr. Yango led his sons into the house. He was very relieved that his sons were safe but at the same time he was worried. The house help served him food but he could not eat. He sat on his favourite chair thinking on the information that the children had given him. His enemy of ten years, Cletus Ngong had brought his children home. He even

76

bought them things to eat on the way back. It was incredible. He wondered whether Cletus had forgotten what had happened between them in high school.

Alice arrived and came into the house looking worried. The look on her husband's face calmed her a bit

'Are they at home?' She asked

'Yes they are.'

'Oh, thank God.' She whispered as he held her chest as if it was about to fall off. At the sound of her voice the two boys rushed out from their room

'Mommy, welcome' Paddy held her hand and led her to a chair. 'Mommy, sit down let me tell you something. Junior's father brought us back from school today. He bought us Yogurt and biscuits. We were very happy. We were waiting for you and daddy to come back home so that we can ask whether we can go and play with junior and Small Mami'

Alice looked at her husband. She remembered his reaction when she had mentioned the visit of Mrs. Ngong, but this was not the time to bring it up. A response had to be made to the children's request. Mr. Yango replied

'That is very kind of him. You do play with them at school don't you?'

'Yes we do, but we can also play at home'

'Let's go and eat Alice' He was not ready to give the children any answer. It was a late lunch and both of them were tired and hungry, but the food was cold so they had to wait for the house help to warm it up. Alice was still wondering about the events of the afternoon and the way the children were reacting. She wanted to make a suggestion to her husband but held her peace. The warm food arrived and they started eating. She watched her husband eat. He always enjoyed his food but this afternoon something was preventing him from eating. He usually finished the quantity of food he put on his plate. He soon sighed and left the table without eating all of what he had dished for himself.

Alice had been hoping that since they had eaten a late lunch, she would not have to prepare supper for her husband. When he left his food half eaten Alice's hopes were dashed to the wall. Alice could not understand her husband's eating habits. He could eat real food at any time of the day or night. When she had asked him about this, he had said it was a carryover from secondary school days when they could soak garri and drink even at 3 o clock in the morning especially when they had serious studies to do. From the exhaustion she saw on his face she knew that he would not go out that evening but he would still eat something before sleeping. Usually when he went out and came back late he usually ate something, as he said to lessen the effect of alcohol on his system. She had come to accept this situation and in order not to disturb her sleep she left the food in a flask on the table from which he served himself.

She too was very tired and looked forward to going to bed early. She had to check the children's work at school that day. This was a routine evening exercise which she shared with her husband. It was his week to check the children's work, but he had gone to bed without doing it. When she eventually left the sitting room and came into the bedroom Bernard was already in his pyjamas and lying between the sheets on the bed. She thought that he was sleeping, so his words not only startled her but also surprised her

'Alice, I think we should go and thank our neighbour for what he did today.

'That's a good idea' Alice replied. She was glad for this change of mind and did not want to seem very anxious for this to happen so she stayed quiet waiting to hear what her husband was going to say again. He said nothing and both of them remained quiet but both of thinking of what had happened that afternoon.

Three days after. Mr and Mrs Ngong were sitting in the parlour watching TV. It was Friday and they were grateful that it was weekend. Since Mr. Che Mba had been transferred to Yaounde, Mr. Ngong missed his company and stayed more often at home in the evenings. He had told her about the Yango kids being abandoned at school. She had been grateful that her husband had not left the children alone at school. She understood that her husband had not done it voluntarily but was happy all the same that he had done it. Now she waited to see what the Yango couple were going to do. She was also thinking about what lay behind her husband's response to her visiting Mrs. Yango and what had triggered his words. She believed that it was not only the insistence of his children that had made him act the way he had done by bringing the children home. She prayed that his action was going to reveal what lay behind this mysterious animosity.

These thoughts were going through her mind when there was a knock at the door. Judith got up and opened the door. She was so surprised that she could not say a word of greeting. Mr. And Mrs. Yango were standing there looking at her. Alice broke the silence.

'Good evening is your husband at home?' she asked. There was all evidence that he was at home because his car was in the garage. Alice just had to say something to break the silence.

'Yes he is, please come in.' Once they were in the sitting room they kept standing until Judith invited them to sit down. Mr. Ngong looked at the couple. Mrs. Yango was a pretty woman. Bernard could not have married any woman less pretty. Cletus thought. Alice sat next to Judith and Bernard after looking around took a seat opposite to where Cletus was sitting

Cletus, whose attention was fixed on the TV set turned his eyes to the door when he heard the knock, but as soon as he realized who his visitors were, he turned his eyes back to the TV and glued them there. Bernard too as soon as he sat down turned his gaze to the TV. He had looked at Cletus briefly as he entered but did not catch his eyes as Cletus had already turned his eyes away. Both men were not seeing what was on the TV screen. What was fixed on Cletus's mind's eye was Bernard's face and what was on Bernard's was the look on Cletus's face when his eyes had alighted on him. Cletus's was a look of superiority and disgust followed by a condescending silence.

For a moment Bernard regretted his decision to come. The women as if pulled together by their shared incomprehension also sat quiet. Their eyes too were on the TV but their ears were alert to what was about to be said. Whatever was amiss was between the two men and they could not interfere until they understood what was happening and if their intervention was called for.

'Hm, hm.' Bernard cleared his throat. He was finding it difficult to talk, but he had taken the initiative to come so he had to continue.

'Cletus.' Cletus turned and looked at him briefly and turned his gaze back to the TV screen. Bernard continued.

'It has been ten years since we left CCAST Bambili, but what happened there all came to my mind as soon as I saw you' Cletus was about to make a retort to this but kept his peace. Judith and Alice looked at each other. They no longer looked at the TV seen but at the two men. Since the women were sitting near to each other and the men were sitting opposite each other, the women had to look from one face to the other by turning their heads from one side to the other. Bernard continued.' We are adults now and I think it is necessary and even unhealthy for us to continue to harbour adolescent hatreds'

Cletus was about to tell him that if he was saying that because he had brought his children back from school then he should forget it because he had not done it out of his own free will, but the look he saw on his wife's face stopped him. The look carried a bit of rebuke, incomprehension and disbelief. Cletus did not like what was happening because he knew that he owed his wife an explanation. Cletus had planned to give Bernard a good dressing down if ever he crossed his path. Now was the time but he was no longer in control neither was Bernard. Other forces had taken over their lives. This was a bitter pill for Bernard to swallow but it was already in his mouth and much depended on his swallowing it. He took the plunge

'We are men now and have other concerns. We have other things on which to expend our energies...'Cletus was becoming impatient. He knew why Bernard had come to see him. He just wanted him to say what he had come to say and leave, so he helped him on.

'Have you come here to thank me for bringing your sons home?'

'Cletus please let him speak' Judith interrupted. Anger at this interruption clouded Cletus's face, but since he wanted to show Bernard that he has always been a gentleman, he wiped it off his face immediately.

'Yes, but that is just part of it. I am an adult now and...'

'So am I.' Cletus had intended his retort to be insulting, but it was lost on Bernard who did not understand the nuance in the response and continued in line with Cletus's statement. 'Yes, we are adults now and should behave like adults and let bygones be bygones.'

Alice realized that the situation was going to deteriorate if left in the hands of the men. She had to interfere.

'We have come to thank you for bringing our sons home from school. As my husband said, that is not the only reason. I am happy that I have a neighbour like Judith. She came to welcome me into this neighbourhood. No woman in the towns where I have lived has ever done so. I appreciate that very much.'

Both men were deflated. Cletus saw the smile on his wife's face and that was enough to soften him. He looked at Bernard. His head was bowed. Bernard the arrogant, Bernard the proud fellow, with his head bowed was a sight. He lifted his head and looked at Cletus right in the eyes. Cletus also looked at him right in the eyes too

'You are a gentleman Cletus' Bernard said and smiled.

Some months later the story of the campaign week in CCAST Bambili was narrated one evening amidst hilarious laughter as both couples sat in the Yango sitting room. Bernard exaggerated the state of drunkenness of his supporters and Cletus description of the fight that night left the women giddy with laughter. In the narration of the story they remembered the names of some of their class mates and wondered what had become of them in life. They knew where a few were, but nothing was known about a majority of them. Reminiscing on the CCAST days took the rest of the evening, but they neither spoke of Bernard's girlfriend jilting him nor the reasons.

Friends

Inoticed Charles before I really met him. There was no way I could not have noticed him. As we waited for our luggage to be sent up the carriage of the bus at the Jeannot Express Bus Service at Sonac Street, Charles was talking with two other boys. The three boys were dressed in Jeans' trousers and tee shirts with the jackets of the trousers flung over their shoulders. They wore white snickers and gesticulated as they talked. They were talking about their exploits in town and the Ayaba Night Club. They had made five papers each a the Advanced Levels Examination from Sacred Heart College Mankon and the celebration of their successes was the centre of their conversation and Charles Parents had even thrown a party for him.

I was from G.H.S Ndu and was dressed in a pair of black trousers with a pullover over my shirt. I wore a pair of brown sandals which had seen many days. I listened to them talking but my attention was focused on Charles who had finesse about him which I could not define.

I was a village boy and had live all my life in the village making very few trips to Nkambe and Kumbo and once to Bamenda. My one-week stay in Bamenda was not enough for me to imbibe life in the township. I was basically a village boy. My success at the Advanced Level and my admission into the University of Buea was my opening into the world.

The bus was finally loaded and passengers were asked Otto take their seats. I hoped that Charles was not going to seat next to me but he did. From the numbers on our tickets the four of us had to sit on the last row of seats in the bus. They continued to talk as the bus sped over the hills heading south. I was seated by the window, which was open. Cold air was rushing in and I enjoyed it. Charles asked me to close the window because the cold would give him catarrh. I closed the window. The inside of the bus soon became too warm as we approached Bafoussam. I dozed off. I might have leaned on Charles for I only felt a push that made me almost hit my head on the window pane.

'Don't lean on me again.' He warned me.

'I am sorry, I did not intend to' I replied. He looked at me for some time and turned away. He was surprised at my reaction. He might have expected me to be defensive or rude. I had the feeling that when he actually looked at me he liked what he saw for he kept stealing glances at me. I took out a novel I had brought along to keep myself company and started reading. The novel was titled 'Dogs of War by Tom Clancy. As soon as I started reading Charles asked me if he could look at the title. I let him have the book. When he read the blurb at the back of the book he said he would like to read the book too.

This was my first time of going to the South West Province and it was like an adventure into the world. I was very proud of myself for going to the University of Buea, which was said to be the place to be. I heard about life at the university and its Molyko neighbourhood from university students who came to the village on holiday. This heightened my sense of adventure and I was ready to take whatever was to come my way as a challenge. I had an uncle who lived in Buea. He had promised me a surprised gift if I had the four papers I had gone in for. This gift turned out to be a room in his mini-cité which was located near the university. That was where I was going to stay.

We arrived Kekem, a small bustling roadside town which owed 80% of its income to the passengers in buses that moved from the Littoral and South West Province to the North West and Western Provinces. The inhabitants of this town are mostly farmers but the number of buses that pass through the town in a day had encouraged the people to open provision stares, on license bas and eating places. The most prominent business activity is the roasting of plantains, mostly ripe ones, cocoyam plum and maize. These are usually eaten with roasted meat popularly known as 'soya'. As each bus slowed down looking for a place to par, hawkers rush after them shouting out their wares. The whole roadside was a cacophony of sights sounds and smells. I looked on the meat displayed on braziers. They looked tempting. Back in the village there were many cattle and meat was not scarce. Meat was relatively cheap but not many families could buy and eat meat on a daily basis. I came from such a family. To us meat was a delicacy and we were brought up not to mind whether we ate meat or not. As children the killing of a chi ken for food was an event we looked forward to, as we would scramble for the entrails to clean out and roast. I looked at the sticks of soya. I wanted to indulge myself, but when I asked for the cost of one stick and was told a hundred francs I lost my eagerness to eat the soya. I did not see myself buying such a tiny quantity of meat for two hundred francs. I had been warned to be careful with my money. Buea was a very expensive town and I was going to be on my own without control from anybody. If I started indulging myself and developing such appetites, things were not going to be easy on my part. I gave up thoughts of eating soya.

Going away from the village to a university so far away was an event. Relatives had come to bid me farewell and had given me gifts of money and foodstuff. On second thoughts this experience was not going to repeat itself so I wanted to make this trip memorable. I had enough money on me. I jumped out of the bus. Charles and his friends had gone out before me. They were eating soya and drinking juice from plastic bottles. I was very hungry and wanted to eat something more solid. That morning in Bamenda I had taken just a cup of tea and a slice of bread. This was very light compared to what I usually ate in the morning in the village. I looked at the roasted cocoyam but thought I would look stupid biting into it. Women were selling cooked food in front of the bars. I did not want to food especially rice for fear of vomiting in the bus. It would be a big disgrace especially with Charles and his friends sitting by me. I moved into one of the bars and asked for a small bottle of juice in a plastic bottle. I was told to pay three hundred and fifty francs. It was too expensive and I thought that an additional fifty francs would get me four sticks of soya. I walked out and got two fingers of roasted plantains for one hundred francs and three sticks of soya. After eating I bought a packet of water for fifty francs and drank. I was satisfied. I went back to the bus. Charles and his friends were waiting outside since I had to get in before them. The bus took off and as it crossed the Nkam River, Charles turned to me and asked.

'Are you going to Buea?'

'I was surprised at his question. All along his friends had behaved as if I did not exist. I could not understand he was talking to me. I did not want to be rude so I responded

'Yes, I am'

'To the university?'

'Yes'

Have you been to Buea before?' I immediately suspected his reason for asking. Maybe he wanted to know if I was an old or new student at the university. Since I knew that they were going to the university as first year students just like me, there was no use to circumvent the matter.

'I have just been admitted into the university.' At my answer Charles face brightened.

' I am also going in as a new student. What are you going to read?'

With my four Advanced Level papers in the sciences I knew that I was going to do something in the sciences. But I was not yet sure. To say that I did not know would me look foolish and destroy the impression I was already creating on Charles. I had asked about the various courses offered in U B in the sciences and had made up my mind but I did not want to reveal this, so I replied.

'There are many courses offered in the various departments. There is going to be a day for orientation to better acquaint the freshmen of the content and prospects of the courses they were going in for'

Charles was quiet impressed by what I had said and stayed quiet for some time. His friends were dozing away. He seemed to be digesting what I had said. I did not want him to continue his questioning, so I opened my novel and continued reading from where I had folded the edge of the page. I did not understand the reason for his interest in me. When we left the Bikoko Junction and was heading west, Charles turned to me again.

'Have you got a room yet?'

His question startled me for although I had a fascinated attraction towards Charles I had a feeling that I would not be comfortable being in his presence for long, yet I wanted to let him know how much I was prepared for the university.

'Yes, I have'

'Where?'

'In a mini-cité ' called 'Shelter'

'Aha, that is where a room has been reserved for me. So we are going to be neighbours.'

I did not reply to this. I was happy about being neighbours with Charles but a nagging thought kept me ill at ease with the idea.

Buses from the Jeannot Express Service carrying passengers from Bamenda to Buea offer door to door services. The volume of cargo passengers bring down from the 'Graffi Country' necessitates this service, so you would find a passenger in one of these buses spending one more hour in Buea before arriving at his destination as the bus had to move from one neighbourhood to the other to off load the luggage of the passengers.

So I found myself sitting only with Charles at the back of the seat when his friends left the bus at the Malingo Street Junction. The bus was now lurching and bumping over the stones and potholes along the Lady 1 Street heading towards the Solidarity Clinic.

I did not bring down the furniture new student's usually brought, for my uncle had a furniture workshop in Great Soppo and had made my bed and chairs there. Clarkes also did not have any furniture with him and I did not ask why. My uncle had set up my room with a bed a reading table and a chair and had left the key with a neighbour. I brought down my mattress. As I carried my things into the room Charles followed me into the room. He was impressed at the way things were moving smoothly for me. His room was still empty and he kept his suit cases there. Many students were still putting up with friends while they waited for the final arrangement for their rooms or for the six month rents to be completed before they were given the keys to their rooms. Charles did not have any of these problems. In fact, his rents for one year had been paid and as he told me later his parents were coming from Yaoundé the next day to buy the things he needed to furnish his room. I had heard of the high cost of living in Buea and I was experiencing it first-hand. From what I had seen of Charles so far I knew that it was not going to be a problem for his parents to buy whatever he needed no matter the cost of these things in Buea. From the type of suitcases he had and he had four of them I knew that he was from a rich family. I wondered what were in the suitcases. Looking at Charles I thanked God for my uncle.

I had to go to my uncle's house as soon as I arrived. It was my first time of visiting him and when Charles with nothing to do offered to come along with me, I dissuaded him. I already had an idea of the figure I wanted to cut in UB and did not want to reduce my chances before I had even started.

Coming to the University of Buea was a breakthrough for me. I was tired of village life. I wanted some excitement. Stories I had heard from university students who came on holiday to the village had thrilled me. Now I was actually there myself and looked forward to living my life the way I thought I had to. I wanted to shed the shell of conformity under which I had lived with my parents. I wanted to be free to go to nightclubs to drink beer and go to places like Limbe and Douala. These are places I had only heard off but now there were not far from where I was. Most important of all I wanted to have a girlfriend, a real girlfriend and not the types in the village, who only wanted money. I had been made to understand that if you are in the university without a girlfriend then you were not a boy. But I was not in a hurry.

I knew that my uncle was going to be a restraining force but he had done so much for me that I did not want to do anything that would turn him against me. I was ready even to leave a double life and never let him know what I was doing, so taking Charles along on my very first visit would have been a dead giveaway.

My uncle lived in Great Soppo. He lived in his own house near the Great Soppo Catholic Church. By the time I got to Street Two it was already dark. I had never seen so many stones in my life. The whole road was covered with stones. The little soil that could be seen seemed to have come there by accident. As I walked along following the directions he had given me I kept my eyes where I kept my feet, yet I still hit the front of my shoes on the stones.

My uncle's hose was a three-bedroom house. It was built with cement block instead of 'Carabout' a local type of plank with which most of the houses are built. For this I was grateful, for I would eventually come with my friends to visit him. The figure I wanted to cut would not have been commensurate with the type of house in which the person who was my closest relative, in fact, my father lived. Where a man lives tells the world a lot about him. My uncle was in the house when I arrived. He was in the sitting room with a friend. He was so happy to see me. He was very proud of me. I could see it in his eyes. Each time he looked at me he smiled even when I was not looking at him. His wife and children came and greeted me. He introduced me to his friend and told him how he was very proud of me. He told him how many papers I had at the Advanced Level and the grades. He was convinced that I was going to be a medical doctor.

My uncle did so much for me because each time he came to the village I was his right hand man. I ran errands for him. When he came home for any celebration I took care of cleaning his compound and setting up the place. I did purchases for him. He trusted me. I was very honest with him and he rewarded me well. I did not see any reason why I should be dishonest with him. He even sent money to me from Buea to do things for him in the village. By doing all he had done was his way of rewarding me for who I was and what I had done to him. When I saw the number of people living with him I was grateful that he had thought of giving me a room of my own near the university. He had four children of his own. The first was in for three, the second in form one, thither two were in the primary school. Two big boys and a girl were also living with him. The boys were apprentices in his workshop. He had bought them from the village so I knew them. The girl was training to be a seamstress and helped in the house work and occasionally went to the farm with his wife. Each of our relatives who went to Buea came back and said they had stayed in uncle Ngalla's house. I could imagine how crowed the house would be when these people came. From the appearance of the upholstered chairs I knew they served as beds.

My presence called for a celebration. After I had eaten he sent for drinks. Back in the village I never drank beer. I was always being told that to drink beer you must be able to afford it yourself because if you got into the habit of drinking it would become an addiction, and if you cannot afford it you will surely fall into evil ways to be able to get what you want. The local drink brewed from fermented corn with a dash of fermented palm wine was more alcoholic than beer and I drank it without any problem and no body complained. Maybe they did not because it was cheap.

My uncle asked what I was going to drink. I said I wanted a bottle of Pamplemousse. He laughed and said that I was a big boy now and could drink beer. I do not know whether he was teasing me or he was serious, but I declined and got my bottle of Pamplemousse. I knew I was soon going to drink beer, but I did not want my uncle to have an idea of what was going on in my mind I wanted him to keep the image of the Valentine he had known in the village.

In three days Charles too was comfortably settled in his room. Much of the furniture in his room was bought in Buea. I envied the things he had in his room. His parents had brought a small refrigerator, a musical set, a table cooker, an electric iron and a plastic carpet covered the floor of his whole room.

I convinced myself that with time I was going to get these things as well.

During the period of registration I hardly saw Charles except in the mornings when I went to his room or he came to mine to ask how far I had gone or when we met somewhere in town. The new students had to go to many offices in town to certify documents needed by the registration office at the university. When this was over they had to make sure that the courses they were offering were counter signed by the authorities of the department concerned. It was a tedious exercise as students had to stand in queues for hours waiting to sign in for the courses. Charles was offering the same microbiology courses as I did, so we often met. The other two boys with whom Charles had travelled were offering different courses, but the three of them were always together when they were free.

When classes finally began the excitement gradually began to dwindle. Some classes began as early as seven o clock in the morning and some took place as late as four o clock in the afternoon. I had to get used to my time schedule. I made a blown up copy of my timetable and pasted it on the wall above my reading table. I was beginning to enjoy my stay in Buea

My uncle soon handed over the collection of the rents for the rooms at the Mini-cité and the settling of water and electricity bills to me. I collected the money paid the bills and gave the rest to him. I was very meticulous in the way I kept my records and he was very happy with me. I had not changed.

Parties characterised the first semester in UB. Many of the ex-student's associations especially those of the mission schools were organizing parties. I was surprised at the frenzy of the preparations. I got to know much about the preparations for the Shesa Party from Charles. He kept me informed of what they were doing. As the preparations went on most of his time was spent attending planning meetings. The party was to take place at the Seme Beach Hotel in Limbe. Charles was a member of the Organizing Committee and had to make several trips to Limbe to contact the hotel authorities and make the necessary arrangements. Because of this he missed some classes but was conscious enough to ask for my notes. He had no time to copy them, not to talk of reading them during this period. He told me he just looked at the subject headings and took note to read them after.

The weekend of the party was approaching and I was surprised when on Wednesday Clarkes asked me whether I wanted to attend the party. I just laughed. I thought he was joking. In my mind I knew that I hadn't twenty thousand francs to pay as gate fee, I was not an ex student of Sacred Heart College, I did not have a suit to wear.

I had watched their preparations with detached interest, but the next day Charles repeated his question. I had a feeling that he was basing his assumption on what I had made him believe about me. I had to tell him the truth without descending from my pedestal. I had quickly picked up the parlance common among students to be able to build up the image of myself which I had in mind. So I replied.

'Mongar, I don't think that is possible'

'Why?' he asked. I could not tell him the real reasons so I had to be evasive. I began with the most obvious

'I am not a Shesan.'

'Friends have been invited and you are my friend.'

'For now I do not have twenty thousand francs for the gate fee' Charles was quiet for some time before asking.

'But do you want to come?' I looked at Charles. He was looking at me straight in the eyes. I saw puzzlement, incomprehension and challenge all assessing me. I had to prove my worth. I could not chicken out. This was the opportunity to prove something to myself. His circle of friends frowned upon my friendship with Charles. Shesans had a world of their own which was quiet distinct. It was difficult for another boy from another school to fit in with them. They could not understand my friendship with Charles. There were times I too wondered what our friendship was all about. I did not spend much time with Charles but since we were neighbours we saw each other often especially in the mornings. He would come into my room to talk with me. In the university and in the Molyko neighbourhood there was so much talk among the students on who was a friend to whom and who was dating who. Charles often surprised me by asking some very deep questions. I call them deep because although they were not out of the normal questions a university boy would ask another, the difference was that Charles took my opinions seriously. He once asked me if I gave money to my girlfriend. When I told him that I did not have a girlfriend, he did not look surprised. He only sighed and said that he wished he were like me. Then he asked me why I had not yet had a girlfriend. I simply said that I had not met anyone yet. My answer sounded so ridiculous that he actually laughed. He could not believe that with so many girls around I had not yet met anyone.

Then he asked if I had a girlfriend I would give her money. I told him that if I had a girlfriend I would not give her money because I am a student just like her and have no source of income.' What about your pocket money'? It was my turn to laugh. 'What I have is not even enough for me?

The party was going to change so much in my life, but at this time I did not know. I had agreed to go to the party. Charles had proved himself an efficient organizer and his friends appreciated his contributions. He made sure that I went to the party, but I still had one problem, no two. I had to get myself an outfit for the party and then I had to brace myself for whatever was going to happen at the party. I had listened to second year Shesans talking about the party of the previous year, but this did not stop the butterflies from fluttering in my stomach. I had never attended such a party. From the frenzy of preparations and the way the boys were talking about it I knew that it was going to be something spectacular. The parties I had ever attended were the ones organised by the students on holiday during the Cultural Week. This party was going to launch me into the type of life I was gradually creating for myself or I was doomed for ever.

The whole of the morning of the Saturday of the party I did not see Charles. He had told me to wait for him at about five p.m. for us to go together to Limbe. The whole day I could not settle down to do anything. I was restless as the time crawled by. I had looked at my limited wardrobe and was undecided as to what to wear. I did not have to wear a suit. I was a guest, but there was a code of dressing which was expected of the guests. One thing I had put up as my next priority after my studies was my dressing. I did not have many pairs of trousers and shirts but those that I had were good and I could mix and match them and always looked well dressed. This habit came to my rescue. I had also discovered that a second hand shirt once given to be technically washed in a pressing was as good as a new shirt. My favourite shirt was check white and brown. I matched it with a brown pair of trousers. When I tried this on the effect was stunning. I had bought a black pair of shoes in Bamenda during my three-day stay there before leaving for Buea.

I was ready for the party physically but emotionally I was not certain. I was in UB and was about to experience one of the two that could make or mar a student's social and academic life. These are the two things that grease the wheels that make life go round in UB. In the absence of one of these the wheel slows down. I am saying this because I was soon to learn the frustration that go with too little social life or too much of it. I was soon to see students hiding behind the screen of religious ardour but at unguarded moments or when another opportunity lends itself, they begin doing just the things they had publicly denounced. I am already straying from my story. Let me tell you about the party.

At six o clock that evening I heard a knock at my door. Charles had come back from Limbe. He looked exhausted. I too had fallen into a shallow sleep when I was tired of waiting. I invited him in but he said we hadn't time to waste because he had to be back in Limbe before eight o clock that evening. With this he went to his room. I was no longer feeling fresh so I went into my bathroom to take another bath. It was a hot afternoon and I wanted to feel fresh. I had heard that Limbe was a very hot place. I wanted to appear calm and fresh. When I heard a knock again I came out. Charles was dressed in a dark suit. I looked at him to detect any sign of disapproval of my attire. He raised his eyebrows and smiled. I did not need words to understand that I was alright. A bus was waiting for us at the road. The bus had come right to the entrance of the Mini-cité so we would not have to walk to the main road. Other boys and girls soon joined us. I was separated from Charles as he had to sit next to the driver. As the bus stumbled in and out of potholes towards Mutengene I studied the boys and girls sitting with me in the bus without appearing to do so. They were talking excitedly about the party. I knew some of them, but after a polite greeting they ignored me. Among Charles friends I was used to being ignore and I never took it to heart. I spoke when I wanted to whether anybody listened and responded or not, but most of the time they responded. I soon attracted the attention of the girls seating next to me. I did not let them know that this was a new experience to me. I have an enormous capacity to remember things and I used what I had heard in my conversation as if I did them all the time.

The party was warming up. The speeches had been made and the buffet table laid out. I listened to the president's speech. If I did not know that he was a third year student, he could have passed for the manager of a parastatal or a director in one of the ministries. The manner with which he spoke, what he said, his dressing and mannerism all had this effect. He exalted and praised their Alma mater, the high expectations from Shesans and the integrity they should maintain. He spoke as if they were a special breed of boys. I now understood the reason for their snobbish attitude.

But Charles was not snobbish towards me. He was not sitting on the high table but at a table near to it so that he could consult with the president. He also had to get up from time to time to see that things were moving well in the room in terms of the food and drinks being served. I had never seen such food before. I ate chicken until it had no taste in my mouth. I had thought that I would eat nothing but chicken, but after the first few slices I lost interest. It was too soft. It was not as tasty as the slices of chicken I occasionally ate in the village. The orderliness that existed in the hall disappeared as soon as the dancing started. The sitting arrangement had been made in such a way that the same number of boys and girls sat on the same table. I found myself sitting on the same table with the girl who had sat by me in the bus. Charles occasionally looked in my direction. I guessed he was looking to make sure that I was alright. When he looked again and our eyes met I gave him the thumbs up sign.

The dancing was in full swing now and I did not lack a partner to dance with. In fact I did not sit down during any one record. Dancing comes easily to me. In the village I was always one of the boys to be chosen to display traditional dances whenever there was an occasion in the palace to entertain visitors. I picked up the 'Dombolo' dance steps and swing and soon was doing it as if I was born with it. The 'Pedale' style of dancing was in vogue and I pushed back my buttocks and twisted to the rhythm of the record.

At one point those dancing near me started to clapping and giving me more space to do the swings. I don't know what got into me. Maybe it was the punch that was served at midnight. My inhibitions had fled out of the window and I was liberated. More boys and girls were coming round and forming a circle with me in the middle. I saw a boy beckoning on me. I immediately understood what he wanted. We do this in the village. I moved towards him took his place and joined the circle while he went to the centre of the circle for his own display. I was actually sweating now. I took off my handkerchief to wipe my face, but before I could do it, the girl next to me had hers out and was wiping my face. I smiled my thanks and she smiled in return.

During a break in the dancing I sat down to catch my breath. I reminded myself not to get drunk, for I was feeling funny. I had drunk two bottles of beer and a glass of 'punch'. I knew that it was the punch giving me this funny feeling. Before the punch was served the president made a comment about it, which I did not take seriously. Now I understood why he had said that. Each person was entitled to three bottles of beer. For my third I took bottle of Pamplemousse to neutralize what I had taken. I really wanted to rest but could not as the girls kept coming to take me for a dance.

By the time we arrived back in Buea at about six am I was completely exhausted with a splitting headache. I came back so late because I had to wait for Charles who had to see that everything was settled with the hotel authorities. I only managed to take off my clothes and crashed on my bed. I got up at one pm with a splitting headache and an aching hunger in my stomach. I went over to my pots and took out the remains of the jellof rice I had cooked the previous day and ate it without heating it. I went back to the bed and slept again for two hours. At three pm I got up, took a bath dressed and went to look for Charles. When I knocked at his door there was no response. I turned the knob and opened the door. He was not in but his bed looked too rumpled for one person to have twisted the sheets that way and a smell hung in the air. I closed the door and went back to my room with the implication of what I had seen dawning on me. With this in mind I could not sleep again.

It was a Sunday afternoon and I wanted to visit my uncle, but I was afraid that he would notice that there was something wrong with me, for I was not feeling myself. I did not see Charles for the rest of the day. The next day was a Monday and we had a class at seven thirty in the morning. I left for classes without seeing Charles. After classes for the day were over, as I was moving home I saw Charles moving home with some boys. I moved over to them. I wanted to thank him for making it possible for me to attend the party, but I could not say this in the presence of the other boys. After greeting them I went closer to Charles and said.

'I came to your room yesterday afternoon but you were not in.' He looked at me for some time before saying

'I went out.' If he was thinking what I was thinking then he did not hide it well. He laughed and said.

'I was so hungry that I went out to look for something to eat'

'I had some jellof rice remaining; you should have come and eaten some.'

'You were still sleeping when I passed by your door.' He answered. By now we had left the other boys and had branched to our own side street that led to our Mini Cite. We were just the two of us now and I could say what I really wanted to say.

'I really want to thank you for all you have done for me especially the party'

'I could see that you were really enjoying yourself'

'Yes I really did enjoy myself'

'Only that you came back alone' I was about to ask him what he meant by that when the girl who had wipe my face during the dance walked up to us.

'Hi Carine!' Charles greeted. 'Meet my friend Valentine. He was our star of the party'

'You do not need to introduce him to me. I know him.'

'I know her too. She is a wonderful dancer' I replied. Charles laughed and said. 'I could see the two of you digging it out. After this I kept quiet.

As I listened to them talk I had a feeling that the conversation was not natural. There was something about the way they spoke that gave me the feeling that they were saying more than I could grasp. Charles did notice that during the party I had danced many records with this girl. She had even accompanied me to my door before moving away with the other boys and girls to their Mini Cite. They continued to talk about the party as we approached the entrance to our Mini Cite. Charles and I had another class at two pm and I wanted to get some sleep before the next class. I did not know whether Carine had another class but I did not ask. We walked together right to our Mini Cite. Instead of Carine moving on to her Mini Cite, she stopped at my door and asked if she could come in. I had nothing to be embarrassed about. My room was neat. When she got in her first comment was

'Your room does not look like that of a boy'

'Why'

'It is too neat'

'Is it a crime for a boy's room to be neat?'

'No, it is a positive point. Very few boys keep their rooms neat like this.' Thanks for the compliment.'

As we spoke she was looking round the room. Her eyes came to rest on the blown-up copy of my timetable pasted on the wall above my reading table.

'You are a serious boy' she observed. I just looked at her. I did not know what to say. I did not understand why she was in my room, but the way she laid half reclined on my bed and the manner with which she was talking intrigued me. I wanted to find out what lay behind all these, so I said.

'You are a beautiful girl.' This did not startle her as I had expected. Instead She smiled and said.

'Really?' I pursued.

'I have not had the opportunity to thank you for wiping my face during the party. Thank you for your concern. I stopped and waited for her response. She did not respond. We were silent for some time.

'Vally, I did that because I like you' I was not surprised at her statement. I had seen it coming. I did not reply immediately. I just looked at her with a smile on my face. She did not look at me. She was looking at the flowers on my bed sheet. Then she lifted her eyes and looked at me. I moved over and sat by her on the bed.

'I like you too Carine' and that is how it all began. Later when Charles heard about my relationship with Carine, he came to my room.

'Vally, how can you do this to me?' he asked.

'What have I done?'

'You and Carine, you hid it from me'

'But you know now.' I laughed to make light of the situation.

'You should have told me'

'Is that something to be discussed? You never discuss your girlfriends with me.' As I said this I looked at him in the eyes remembering the afternoon after the party when I had walked into is room

'It is all right. I just thought that you should have let me know.'

'I also thought that by now you should have seen it for yourself.' I replied.

'It's okay' he said. 'That's better for you.' The way he said it gave me the impression that he had me where he wanted me to be.

Classes were on now seriously. I had not lost sight of my priorities and was concentrating on my studies. Carine was my major distraction. She came to my room when I did not expect her. She waited and accompanied me to my room after classes. I did not like this because after class I liked to rest and go over what had been taught that day for it to stick to my brains. I had discovered this about myself right from form three. After the lessons of each day I took time to go over them again.

But Carine was disturbing this habit. In her presence I could not take up my books to read. I liked her and enjoyed her company.

Charles often came to my room for us to discuss some topics in the course work. Our friendship had reached the

103

level where he just assumed that whatever help he needed in his studies I was there to give him. I did not resent this. Writing the A Levels had taught me that what mattered was what you eventually wrote down during the examinations.

I was spending more and more time with Carine. Once she had come in when Charles and I were discussing a topic we had been sent to do some research on. Before I could tell her that were busy, Charles was already packing his books to go away. I was angry and confused. I did not know whether to be angry with Charles or with Carine.

It was the first week of December and the Christmas period was fast approaching but its effect was low-keyed on Campus. This was a dangerous period because immediately after the Christmas break the first semester examinations began. Every student knew about it but as Christmas came nearer students started thinking of home and the festivities of this period.

The euphoria of Christmas in town was spilling over to the campus. Many students were engaged in practicing the singing of carols in the various Christian groups to which they belong. Some went to weddings which are usually celebrated at this time of the year. Some went on drinking sprees or visits to neighbouring towns. From the way the first year students in particular were bent on enjoying themselves, it looked as if there would never be another opportunity of this sort.

It was common knowledge among the students that one's performance in the first semester test would act as an indicator of what would come later. Failing a course at this early stage was not a good sign. I was determined not to start accumulating this academic baggage so early, but I could not resist the temptations of this period.

Carine was very much part of my life now. I liked the way she behaved. I liked the girls who were her friends. I began to trust her. She made no demands on me. She was level headed and had the same academic concerns as I did. One Saturday morning I heard a knock at my door when I was still lying in bed. I opened the door and found Carine standing there. Just looking at her, I knew that there was something wrong.

'Come in Carine, What is the matter?' She did not respond as she came in and sat on my reading table chair. 'What is it Carine? 'I asked again as she continued to be silent.

'After a sigh she said

'I am sorry to bother you Vally, but you are the only person I can turn to for help. It is two months now that I have not been able to pay my water and electricity bills. My Landlord came yesterday and made a lot of noise about it. My father promised sending me money last weekend. I do not know what has happened. Please give me ten thousand francs. I will give you back as soon as my father sends me the money.

I was already familiar with this issue of collecting money for rents, water and electricity bills. It was the boys who gave a lot of trouble to the Landlords. The girls always paid their bills. I thanked God that the tenants under my care were not difficult. I tried to be friendly and understanding with them. I had no reason to be rude to them or unusually hard, but some landlords and caretakers of Mini Cites were impossible, so I understood what Carine was going through.

I had just collected some money for electricity and water bills and some outstanding rents which I had not yet handed over to my uncle. I was very careful how I kept the money I collected. So far there had not been any incident of theft. I was quite away of the rampant incidents of theft in the student's residential areas. A room left unguarded for five minutes was a target. Radios, compact Discs, gas bottles, clothing and shoes have been stolen from students by other students. Cell phones were the main targets. I hid the money I collected in very unlikely places. I had learnt this from my father who hardly sent us u\into his room to look for something without telling us exactly where it could be found. I told Carine to go back to her room; I was going to see what I could do. I did not want even her to see where I hid the money. Thirty minutes later, I was knocking at her door. I had all confidence that she was going to give me the money as soon as she got it

I was Charles's closest friend now. Although the other two boys were still his friends because they were Shesans, I was the one who related to him on a day to day basis. The fact that we were offering the same courses kept us together much of the time.

Charles enjoyed going to parties and could not miss any opportunity that came his way. The Saint Augustine Ex-students' Association had organized a party at M& g Night Club in Buea. The intricate pattern of relationships at the university accounted for the heterogeneous nature of these parties. This was one I did not want to miss. After the party in Limbe I got to know so many boys and girls. I was usually pointed out to others as the boy who had displayed at the Shesan party in Limbe. Tosses who did not know me thought that I was a Shesan. I did not mind this but I was careful not to get myself into a position of ridicule. I let them believe what they wanted to.

106

The night of the party found Carine and I at the M&G Night Club. Charles was also present with his girlfriend and other boys and their girlfriends. Though the setting was not as sophisticated as the nightclub of the Seme Beach Hotel in Limbe, the atmosphere was the same. The nightclub had been booked so only those who presented an invitation at the gate were allowed in. Many of the university boys came with their girlfriends. Others did not but there was no law that prevented any of them from dancing with the girls. This was a potentially dangerous situation and this happened to me.

My uncle had given me some latitude in using some of the money I collected from to tenants. I made sure that I did not go above a certain amount which I thought reasonable. When he did not complain when I told him what I had done with the money he never complained. Some of the things I told him were not true, but this did no harm. I was getting to be at ease when I used money. The panic reflex which I had each time I used more money than I should have was gradually fading away because I knew that with my uncle I would never lack anything as long as I was the valentine he has always known. With this assurance I became careless. I had taken along the sum of twenty thousand francs. After paying the gate fee of five thousand francs each for Carine and me were left with ten thousand francs which I thought would take us through the night. I did not intend to drink much. I had come to dance and once more display my skills.

Dancing seemed to intoxicate me. The more I danced the more I wanted to dance. I had started to drink beer but that night Charles discouraged me from drinking beer. He said that it made you pee too often. I agreed with him I had noticed that when I drank too much I went out often to ease myself. He advised me to drink Whisky Black but before he said this I had taken a bottle of Export Beer. I was surprised at my capacity to drink beer. I believed this was because my system was used to the alcohol in the local drink we consumed at home. I had set my limit to three bottles of beer. After drinking he first bottle of Whisky Black, I felt elated. The DJ at the nightclub was superb. He knew what records appealed to us. I danced with many other girls but more often with Carine. She also danced with other boys, but when she was dancing with one boy I noticed that they were arguing. I did not know what was happening. I was not yet into Carine to the extent that I would go intervening or feeling jealous that she was talking with another boy, but what the boy did next pushed me to the wall. The series of records ended and Carine moved back to her seat. I could see that she was not happy. I took her for the next dance and tried to find out what had happened to change her mood. I could not pretend that I was not inquisitive to know what she had been discussing with the boy. I was holding her close when I felt a hand on my shoulders.

'Excuse me please,' the boy said. 'This is my girl. You should not be holding her that close. The fact that you brought her here does not mean that she is yours'

I turned round to look at who was speaking to me. My face came close to that of the boy who had earlier been speaking with Carine. I had never seen her so angry.

'Will you keep away Lawrence? Stop interfering in my life. I have nothing to do with you' she held my hand and led me away from the boy and continued to dance, bit the night was spoiled for me. I could not let myself be carried away by the music after what had happened. I was embarrassed and afraid. I never knew that I could face such a situation in my life. I was not actually fighting with Lawrence over Carine but

I did not like the incident. Carine had handled the situation so well that not many dancers had noticed what was going on. A few minutes after I had sat down Charles came to sit by me.

'What was all that about?' he asked.

'I do not know. That boy says Carine is his girlfriend'

'Do you believe him?'

'I do not know what to think. I have to find out from Carine herself.'

'Do you think that she will tell you?' Charles asked.

'Why not? Is there something you are hiding from me Charles?'

'If I had anything to tell you I would have done so. There is nothing I am hiding, but I think that that boy is up to something. Put an end to it, Vally. I know that Carine loves you. That boy just wants to cause trouble.

'But Charles, there must be something to it. The boy could not have spoken like that if there was no truth in it'

'Vally, be a man. Do not allow such things to weight you down' I did not respond to this and Charles moved away and came back with a bottle of Whisky Black.

'Take this and cool your temper. As I said put an end to it' He went away and as if by arrangement Carine came to sit by me.

'Vally, I am sorry at what happened. I wanted to assure you that Lawrence is just trying to cause trouble between us' I was too angry and confused to say anything. She continued 'I can see that you are still angry with me. I did not want to come and sit by you because I wanted you to calm down. I was angry too and wanted to work out my anger. Now we are both calm and we can now listen to each other.'

'I have nothing to say Carine. Just leave me alone.'

I cannot believe what you are saying Vally. I think Lawrence planned to get you angry this night and you are allowing him to succeed. Let's go and dance'

'No Carine. I do not feel as dancing. But you are angry. Do not allow yourself to be affected by little things like this.'

'Was that a little thing?'

'Yes it was. Have I ever done anything to make you suspicious?' Have you ever seen me with Lawrence? There was all sincerity in her voice and I believed her.

'Okay, just go on dancing, I will join you later' I took my bottle of Whisky Black and joined the other boys who were standing at the counter.

'That's my man,' Charles remarked as soon as he saw me. Peck up man! Peck up!' We both started laughing. He continued. 'Enjoy yourself man, enjoy yourself' and I did.

I was soon dancing again and enjoying myself. This time I held Carine in my arms with all confidence and possessiveness. I do not knower haw it happened but I found myself with another bottle of Whisky Black. By four thirty in the morning we were all ready to go back to our rooms. I was not in the state to be responsible for whatever would happen. We moved out of the dance hall and the sharp cold morning air slapped me in the face momentarily bringing ma back to my senses. The sudden cold was a jolt to the heat of my body. I tried to control myself from the clashing effect of the alcohol and the cold. As we waited for taxi to take five of us to Molyko, Charles tapped me on the shoulders and said 'Look at that fool.' I turned round and saw Lawrence standing a few metres away from us. I moved over to him and said.

'Don't ever make that mistake again' That was all I Intended to tell him. Before I turned away I felt a slap on my

110

jaw. I turned round and gave him a blow on the face and he crashed to the ground. I did not know that the boy would go down so easily. I did not stay to see what was going to happen. I had made my point. Charles and Carine were already leading me away as Lawrence's friends came to help him to his feet.

The slap had cleared my mind of the fogginess of alcohol and I saw exactly where I had placed myself. I was I drunk and involved in a brawl over a girl. What was I going to tell my uncle if he heard and came asking? I was more worried because. The nightclub was in the same neighbourhood were my uncle lived and some boys university students also lived there. Moreover whatever sensational things that students did was always the talk of the town. I was so scared of the fact that my uncle would hear of it. I was also afraid of what Lawrence was going to do afterwards because if I were in his shoes that would not be the end of the story. When I thought of the situation deteriorating into a fight and the police getting involved I shivered with apprehension. I was scared of the stories that were going to be told about me among the students. I hated drawing negative attention to myself. I was afraid for my future. I was agonizing over things that had not yet happened.

Fortunately the two groups of friends had prevented us from attacking each other again. I was particularly grateful because I wanted everything to end, even if it meant ending my friendship with Carine. I was ready to do so not to get myself into such circumstances again.

As soon as we got into the taxi, the fogginess in my head returned as if it was just giving me a reprieve to see exactly where I had landed myself. I felt Carine's comforting arms round me as the taxi sped down to Molyko, I passed out. I

111

tried to open my eyes and they closed on their own. I was not in possession of my body. I was soon aware of lying on a bed but did not know where I was. I was only conscious of drifting off into the arms of a warm comforting sleep.

When I gained consciousness and enough strength to open my eyes I realized that I was not in my room. I was alarmed. I wanted to be wide awake to examine my surroundings but a splitting headache invaded my consciousness. I was grateful for the warm comforting arms and breath that pulled me back into slumber, but I was conscious enough to know that I was naked for I could feel the cold on my body, and someone was lying and snuggling up to my back. I welcomed this warm lethargy and wished I could remain like this forever for deep in my consciousness I knew that there was something wrong and was not ready to face it.

Nature's method of easing the mind and body from stress does not last forever. I got up feeling sick. My mouth was dry like paper and my throat and head ached with a throbbing pain. With the heat in the night club the Whisky Black that I had drunk was cold and this had inflamed the glands on my throat. I had noticed this type of inflammation once when I had sucked on three lumps of 'alaska' a locally made ice cream. I had had a bout of fever that had kept me in bed for a week. My throat had ached and I could not swallow anything. The symptoms were the same and I knew I was in for bout of fever. From the way I was feeling I knew that this one was going to worse than the other.

It was a Sunday and I had to visit my uncle. He was expecting me, but what worried me most was what must have happened during the six hours that Carine and I were in her

112

room. When I got up and realized that she too was naked, I could not look at her. I did not want to look at her face. I did not want her eyes to meet mine. I did not know how I was going to get back to my room in this state.

'Vally, Chei! You can sleep! You have been sleeping as if you will never get up' I did not give a response to this. 'Why are you holding your head like that? Do you have a headache? Let me give you some water and pain killers' She got up from bed. She put on her nightgown and as moved to get the water, I watched her through my fingers and could see her body through the fabric of the gown, which was transparent. I felt a sensation in my loins and my manhood responded. I had never been this close to a woman and my apprehension of what must have happened increased.

'Here is the water and the tablets. When I came back I took some myself but you were already so fast asleep and there was no way I could get you to drink some. When you got up I forgot to give you and you fell asleep again.' She stopped. I wished she could stop talking. All I wanted to do was to get back to my room and continue to sleep, but she continued

'It was not bad. Next time it will be better.' This jolted me out of my slumber.

'What was not bad?' I asked

'So you did not know what you were doing? That is why I say it was not bad' I had a momentary feeling of elation. I had finally done it. Then the feeling evaporated leaving in its place apprehension and anger. I felt I had been used. I was frightened.

'Where are my clothes? I must get back to my room.'

'Take a bath and eat something before you go'

'No I want to go'

'Don't be silly, Vally, I know that you are hungry and there is no food in your room. Do you know what you look like? It is quite a distance from here to your room'

Her arguments were reasonable and I lay back on the bed. The first wave of fever hit me and I shivered.

'Let me heat up some water for you to take a bath. Then I will prepare some garri for you to eat then you can go to your room.'

The hot water gave me some strength. My trousers and shirt were on a hanger and I got dressed, but when I sat down to eat I could not swallow anything. My throat ached and I felt exhausted.

On my way back to my room I walked as leisurely as I could to give any onlooker the impression that I was just taking an afternoon stroll, but I was dying to lie down. As I opened my door I noticed a white sheet of paper pushed into my room. I picked it up and opened it. I recognized my uncle's handwriting and folded it and put it in my pocket without reading it.

'What is it Vally, Who has written it? ' Carine who had accompanied me asked. I did not answer. I knew that whatever was in the letter was not going to be pleasant for my uncle was expecting me in his house with money I had collected for rents. Now was two o'clock in the afternoon. I was already thinking of what to tell him but now that he had come himself the situation was worse. Carine had not yet given me the money she had borrowed, and I had used ten thousand more from the money I was supposed to use. I was thirty thousand francs short of the money I was supposed to give him. I was now more worried about how I was going to explain the shortage than with my illness. I lay down on my bed with my clothes on. The headache had not abated and the fever was coming on strong. I groaned and Carine touched my forehead.

'My God! Vally, you are hot! You have a high fever. I cannot leave you alone.

'No, Carine, you must go. I want to sleep. So there is no need for you to sit here.'

'You are not serious Vally. Do you think that I will leave you alone when you are sick?'

'I am not a baby Carine. I will be alright. It's just the effect of the cold last night. I will be fine. Please just go. You need to rest too. Tomorrow is school'

'The tone of my voice must have made her to understand that I was not just being considerate, I really wanted her to go.

'All right, Vally, I will go but I will check on you in the evening.

'That will be fine.'

I would have wanted Carine to stay with me, but I was afraid that my uncle would come to look for me and would find a girl in my room. This would be catastrophic. When Carine left I got up and locked my door. I remembered the note my uncle had written and pushed under my door. I got it out and it read.

Valentine, I have been waiting for you since midday. Where are you? Come to the house as soon as you come back.'

The letter was not acknowledged, but I knew that he was the one. The question 'Where are you? jolted me. My absence at his house indicated I was where I was not supposed to be. The last statement was a command which I could not obey at that moment.

The fever was fully on now and I shivered in my blanket. I was too sick now to bother about the event of the previous night or my uncle's reactions. I was grateful when sleep over took me.

I cannot remember for how long I slept but a persistent knocking brought me back to reality. From the way the knocking suddenly stopped I knew that the person had been there for a while. I struggled out of bed expecting to see my uncle. Instead I saw Charles's retreating back. When he heard the door opening he turned round and came back.

'Vally, you don't look good at all. Are you sick?' I tried to respond but I could not speak. I just held my throat and shook my head in acceptance. He moved closer and touched my forehead.

'You have a serious fever. You are very sick. It shows even in your eyes. Have you taken any medicine?' I again shook my head in the negative. Charles got up and moved round the room and came and sat down again by my side. I could see that he was worried and I wondered why. He continued 'Do you have any pain killers' I again shook my head in the negative. He got up went to his room and came back with some capsules.

'Drink this. By morning if you do not feel better we would have to go to the Solidarity Clinic. I was not in the state to refuse anything that could relieve me of the pain in which I was, but swallowing the capsules was the problem. When I finally swallowed them they subbed on the inflammation sending a searing pain into my head. After his ordeal I lay back on the bed. Charles sat by me on the bed. We did not speak and I was grateful for his presence and silence. We were silent for quite a while. I prayed that Charles should not speak about Carine. I was not in the situation and

116

mood to think about girls not to talk about them. I was in such a precarious state emotionally that I did not want to think about anything. I did not want to think about my fight with Lawrence. I did not want to think about what must have happened between Carine and me. I did not want to think about what my uncle might be thinking. I did not want to think about the next day. I was concerned with now, and now was the pain I was feeling in my throat.

I was drifting off to sleep when there was another knock on the door. I waited with dread for Charles to open the door. My face was turned to the wall so I could not immediately see who was coming in. I expected to hear my uncle's voice asking why I was in bed. Instead I heard Carine's voice.

'Thank god you are here Charly. I have been wondering what was happening to Vally. I have brought him something to eat.

I did not turn round Carine came round the bed and sat looking at my face. Charles was sitting by my right side and Carine was on the left. I was in the middle. My friends were with me when I needed them most. They were showing their concern about my wellbeing. They were now my family.

'I have brought you some pepper soup with spaghetti. I know that you cannot swallow anything solid' since I could not respond, I held her palm and squeezed it. Charles informed her.

He has just swallowed some capsules with difficulties. I am sure his throat must be on fire. I turned half way round and also held Charles's palm and squeezed it. 'I lay back on the pillow feeling a bit relieved with Charles and Carine on both sides of me. They started talking about the events of the previous night. They talked about it with such light heartedness that it all looked so funny. When they came to the part when I knocked Lawrence down and described how he fell I actually smiled in spite of the pains. As I listened to them talk my headache gradually lessened, but the pain in my throat remained. I enjoyed their company.

While I lay on my bed that afternoon I drifted in and out of sleep. When I was awake I thought of many things. I regretted the situation in which I found myself. In addition to my night out at M& G and the things that had happened there, I had spent much more money from the rents I had collected than I was allowed to. How was I going to explain this expenditure? If news of my fight got to my uncle, what explanation was I going to give? I was sure that he would jump to the conclusion that I have been giving his money to my girlfriends. If he ever met Carine in my room, how was I going to explain her presence? What Had Carine meant when she had said it was not bad? My subconscious was gradually yielding what it had in its depth. I remembered the warm sensation I had felt as I had held Carine in my arms but I could not remember how far I had gone. What if I had gone far enough to have sex without protection? All these thoughts had tormented me as I battled with my throbbing head and throat. I blamed all that had happened to me on Charles and Carine. If I had never known Charles all of these would not have happened. I felt bitter and angry. My friendship with Charles had led me into trouble. My relationship with Carine had made me to be indiscreet with the manner in which I had spent money. I had decided to ask Carine to give me the money she had borrowed. If she did then I would be able to explain away the other expenditure though this meant doing without the things I was planning to say I had used the money to buy. I was going to begin avoiding Charles I thought I had not gained anything from him. I had to stop what I was doing and not allow Charles and Carine to influence me again.

But as I listened to them talk that evening, I felt better. I was participating in the conversation though I did not say much. I looked at their faces as they spoke. I listened to the innuendoes in what they said. As I listened to them I realised a whole new world opening to me, the world of friends. This world, my uncle would never understand. I felt a bonding which I could not explain. They talked about their studies, their dreams, their fears and uncertainties. They spoke about their families but in general terms. I was grateful that I could not speak, for, what would I have said about my parents? Both of them had been born and bred in town. Their parents were civil servants. Thanks to my uncle. I owed my education to my uncle. He had not only financed my education he was the major inspiration behind my zeal to excel academically. In moments when he was very happy with me he would call me his director. He hoped that one day I will become a director, a director of what, I could not say, but this made me to know that if I worked hard at my studies I would become someone important in future. Being a director was being someone important. I was with friends who had the same vision.

I then realized that I did not have to work too hard to be who I wanted to be among my friends. I also realised that I had been suffering from an inferiority complex.

Lawrence was far from my thoughts but when Carine started talking about him, I was consoled by the manner in which she spoke. She did not run him down. She just said that he was suffering from delusions. She cannot understand how he came about with the notion that she was interested in him. They had happened to have sat together in class one day and had walked back home after the class. All the questions I had planned to ask her dissolved in my mind. They were doing everything to make me feel good, that was what I really needed at that moment.

'You must eat before I go Vally' Carine interrupted the conversation. She moved over to the table where she had kept the small flask she had brought. She took out two plates from my small cane Cupboard and dished out the pepper soup. She gave one plate to me and the other to Charles. She ate from the flask because I had just two plates. There was silence for a moment in the room as we sipped the hot delicious pepper soup and the spaghetti slipped down our throats. Each swallow I took was an ordeal as the pepper in the soup made my throat to burn more and I grimaced with pain.

'The pepper will make the inflammation heal faster'

Carine tried to encourage me to eat more. On hearing this Charles almost choked as he tried to control the act of swallowing and laughing at the same time.

'What type of prescription is that Carine? The pepper will make it worse.'

'My mother told me that pepper makes wounds heal faster. When she has a cut on her finger she does not put any medicine on it for it to heal.'

'But she does not put pepper on it' Charles reminded her'

'But she grinds pepper whenever she is cooking and uses her fingers

'Oh girls and their mothers' Charles remarked.

"Yes, God made us what we are so that you can enjoy what we can produce just as you have just done.'

120

While she took the plates away the argument on the healing properties of pepper was still going on and Carine was standing her grounds. We laughed at what she was saying not because she sounded stupid or that we disagreed with what she was saying, her conviction of what her mother had told her was so amusing. Moreover, it seemed they wanted to keep the atmosphere light for my sake.

The atmosphere was so comfortable and relaxing that I wondered what I could have done if I did not have friends like Charles and Carine. All the negative thoughts I had had about them were wiped away. I came away with a new realization. I arrived at certain decisions. In one evening, I had matured. I was better prepared to face the challenges of university life and all it entailed. I was better placed to face the challenges of being a teenager and getting what I wanted. The fright that settled at the bottom of my stomach each time I thought of my uncle's reaction if I got myself into any unpleasant situation was wiped away. I was ready now to face him not as an equal nor as a child, but as a boy who knew what he wanted out of life. On the surface it looked as if Charles and Carine had led me to this realization but deep down in me I knew that this was what I had always longed for.

Before drifting off to sleep when they left I thought of Carine and knew that one day very soon I was going to ask her what she meant by my not doing badly. After raking my memory to find out what must have happened that night I was convinced that I had not gone far enough.

My Mother

I Came home on a Thursday, after writing my last paper of the GCE Ordinary Level Examination. My mother came to take me home. Usually, it was my father who brought me to school and at the end of the term he came and took me home. I was so pleased to see her. I loved to see her driving the car. The family had one car and it was my father who always drove it. Once in a while my mother drove it. This occurred when my father was out of town or when he had one reason or the other to sit at home while my mother used the car to run her errands or go to a meeting. She also occasionally took the car to the market or to church.

Each time I saw my mother driving the car it assured me that she was capable of doing things on her own. My father had made her so dependent on him that she could do nothing without telling him, asking his advice or just to let him know. Whatever her motive was or her expected outcome of a situation she wanted to handle, it always boiled down to what he wanted or what he approved of. That afternoon she came to take me home she was glowing with some inner joy I could not understand.

Since I was in a mission secondary school, I was away from home for most of the year. When I was at home on holyday I did not like the role my mother played in the family. It seemed as if her whole existence was based on pleasing my father or avoiding displeasing him.

She had gone to high school and obtained the Advanced Level in two papers, but her number of points did not permit her to get admission into the University of Buea. She could have gone to the University of Yaounde, Dschang or Douala, but since her parents were living in Buea, they had hoped that she would stay at home and attend the university. All her hopes of going to the university were dashed when her parents told her that they had no money to send her to any of the other universities. My father happened to have gotten into her life during her second year at home and that was the end of it, but she never stopped reading.

My mother came to take me home that afternoon because my father had gone to Yaounde on mission. When we got home she helped me unpack my clothes and arranged them in the wardrobe. She was in very good spirits. I wondered why.

Friday came and passed. I helped her with the house chores and taking care of my two younger brothers and sister. Each time that I was at home I helped her so that she could have more time to rest and read. I once asked her why she read so much when she had no opportunity to put her knowledge to use. It was a daring question but I wanted to hear what she was going to say about it. She was a quiet and easy going woman. I thought that my question was going to earn me a rebuke but she just looked at me and smiled.

On Saturday morning she told me that I was going to accompany her to a 'Njangi' Party that evening. I had witnessed such Njangi Parties' when my parents were the hosts and I was on holyday. The members of the Njangi were men and woman of all walks of life. There were business men, doctors, teachers, lawyers and a few government officials. The two times I had witnessed this event in our home, my mother had a variety of dishes to prepare. A few of her friends and neighbours came to help her. Our own work was to do the odd jobs of plucking the chicken and washing the used pots and bowls to be reused. When all the food had been cooked and put into food flasks to keep them warm, we did general cleaning. We mopped the floor and got the serving dishes plates, glasses and cutlery ready.

During these evenings my mother was so exhausted that she hardly danced or drank as the other women were doing. She was always on the alert to see that her guests had what they wanted. My father did not help in making things easy for her. He complained about one thing or the other. I usually felt pity for my mother, for she would do everything not to appear hurt and to maintain a happy look, but it was there in her eyes. When she thought that no one was watching her, when she let down her guard, this cloak of weariness and suppressed anger would cloud her face.

But this evening we were going to just enjoy ourselves. There was no work to be done. I waited anxiously for the evening to come, but my anxiety had an edge of uncertainty. I had never known my mother to go to a party without my father. She usually went out with him. When they did I have sometimes seen them come back in total silence. On such occasions I always sensed that they had quarrelled. My mother had such an expressive face that one could easily know how she felt just by looking at her face.

When I was ready for the party that evening, I waited for her to call for me when she was done. I waited in my room. She soon called for me and I went out expecting to find her in the sitting room, but she was still in her bedroom. I knocked and went in.

I had never seen my mother looking so beautiful. She had on a red dress with black and silver trimming at the neckline, the sleeves and the hemline. In spite of her four deliveries she had managed to keep a trim figure and the dress hugged her body giving it a youthful shape. Her hair had been pulled to the top of her hair and some artificial hair attached to it and this cascaded down her back with some tendrils of it framing her face. When I came in she used her fingers to brush some tendrils away from her face.

The neckline of her dress was cut low and a gold plated necklace that looked like a golden snake circled her neck. On her ears were matching earrings. When I came in she was looking at her reflection in the mirror and did not see me. This gave me a good time to look at her. What I saw was her reflection in the mirror. When she noticed my presence she turned round and said.

'Come let me see your dress.' I moved closer to her. She had on an exquisite perfume. I could not believe that this was the mother I knew. She had trimmed her eye brows and had applied some eye shadow. Her lip stick was red to match her dress. I did not know that she had such knowledge of colour combination and applying make-up. The whole effect was stunning. I wondered what my father would have said if he had seen her. She did not notice the way I was looking at her.

'That dress looks nice but you need something more stylish. You are a big girl now. Next academic year you will be going to high school.' She paused and took my face into her palms. 'Where is this pimple from?' she asked for, I had not noticed it. 'It will soon go away' she continued. 'Your face is smooth enough. There are no signs that you will have a pimply face. I had applied some Vaseline on my lips. She continued talking 'This is good. It is not yet time for you to start putting on lips stick'

We soon got into the car and took off. She drove carefully. I kept throwing glances at her face, taking note of the changes in her countenance when an oncoming vehicle flashed its light for me to be able to see her face. As I looked at her face I wondered what was going on in her mind. We drove across town to the GRA neighbourhood in Buea. It was quite a long drive from Molyko. When we got to the Great Soppo Market, progress was slow as some of the traders were still by the roadside with their wares packed in cartons looking for taxis to take them back home. When we got to Bongo's Square, she slowed down as if she was deciding on which road to take. The she drive straight on. She got to the Police Roundabout and turned left and took the road to Bokwango.

My mother was not a very communicative person, communicative in the sense of joking with the children or sharing in their confidences. She spoke to us as mothers do; scolding, advising, instructing, warning, sanding us on errands etc. I think she spoke with us the children more than she spoke with her husband. Since I was away most of the time it seemed to me as if she never spoke.

I had always wanted to talk with my mother. I had so much to tell her. I had so much to ask her. There were so many things that I wanted to know. I was a teenage girl and there was so much about my mother that puzzled me. I had never seen her so light hearted. This was my opportunity but I had to be careful.

'Mother, you look so beautiful and happy. I wish you were always like that.'

'Why do you say that? I am always happy. She replied.

'No, mother, I have seen you looking sad. Most of the time you just look a type.'

'Yes my daughter, the outside is not the inside.'

I waited for her to continue but she did not. Her mood did not change; she still had that glowing expression on her face. I wondered at what was going on in her mind. I also wondered what she meant by her last statement.

We arrived at our destination and got out of the car. There were many other cars packed in the yard. We walked into the sitting room. The chairs had been arranged against the walls and many other chairs brought in to accommodate more people. The centre of the room was left clear of any furniture. Men and women were seated and chatting. Some were standing on the veranda. My mother gave a general greeting and led me to a seat but did not seat down herself. She moved off to the dinning section and stood talking with a woman. I guessed that the woman was the lady of the house. As I looked at my mother talking and interacting with the men and women I felt proud of her.

While my mother was away talking with the members of the' Njangi' a man came in and sat on the chair next to me. I almost told him not to, for it was for my mother, but I held my peace. My mother soon came back and sat by the man. She introduced me to the man and we greeted each other. I was not comfortable with the man sitting between us but my mother did not mind.

The events began with a word of prayer and welcome from the host. The ladies were led to the table to take their food. My mother made sure that she stood behind me to watch what I was doing. Maybe she thought that I was going to be shy and not take enough food for myself. I took the amount of food I thought I could eat. I was tempted to take more than two slices of chicken. I actually took three. When I threw a brief glance at the plates of the other people and realised that they had heaped their plates, I thought an extra slice of chicken for me was enough to strike the balance.

Once we had eaten our food, dancing began. To open the floor my mother was paired with the man sitting with us. My mother loved dancing and she danced well. I could not take my eyes off her as she danced.

Before the dancing began my mother was conversing with the man whose name I got as Mr. Paul. I intended listening to what they were saying, but I was also interested in watching the couples dancing on the dance floor, so my attention was divided. What soon caught and held my attention was my mother saying.

'I have read that too.'

'From that moment though I kept my face turned away from them, watching the people dancing, my ears were tuned to what they were saying. I wanted to hear what she was telling the man about what she had read. They delved into a discussion of Tom Clancy's novels and those of John Grisham. These were novels I had never read but had seen them lying in the sitting room or on the dining table or on her bed. She encouraged us to read but I was frightened of such large books. I concentrated on reading love stories and even these were not many. I had my school books to attend to. I listened to my mother narrate the storyline and dissected the characters. Her English was perfect. I could not believe what I was hearing. As she spoke the man looked at her with admiration.

Dancing was going on as they continued to speak. I concluded that she was more interested in the conversation than in the dancing. She soon got up to dance and the man joined her. She danced with abandon. She was enjoying herself. She looked really happy. I danced a number of records with some of the men. They soon knew who I was and asked me about school and the just ended GCE examinations. My answers were brief. They must have attributed my behaviour to shyness, but I was confused. I was confused by the many questions that were going on in my head. When Mr. Paul asked me for a dance, I became more confused. As we danced, I made sure that I did not look at Mr. Paul's face. I noticed that he was looking at me.

'Your mother is a very intelligent woman.' Mr. Paul suddenly remarked. This increased my confusion. Who was Mr. Paul? I wondered. His statement took me unawares and the questions that were in my mind came on strong. I wonder how my mother was going to react and what she would say if Mr. Paul asked her where she worked. This had always been her problem. It was not the financial aspect that bothered her. My father provided well for the family. It was the sense of not being productive, to be able to do something by herself for herself. She felt incomplete because she did not leave the house to go out and do something with the talents and knowledge she had acquired in school. She did not know that what she was contributing to the family was invaluable. Just being there for us was so much. That is how I saw it then. Later in life when I wondered how my mother had borne it all with such serenity, my respect and admiration for her increased. I now understood what she was losing and how she tried to make up to it by satisfying something in her inner self which nobody could comprehend.

Mr. Paul had made a statement not asked a question, but I felt obliged to make a response.

'Really?' It was out of my mouth before I could think about it. It sounded so false. How could I respond like that to a statement about my mother as if I did not believe what had been said about her?

'Yes, she is. She surprises me with how much she knows' I turned to look at my mother. She was looking at us and smiling. I smiled and turned my face away.

On our way back Home I was still puzzled at what had happened that evening. I had the impression that My mother had met Mr. Paul before that evening. I did not want to spoil the evening for her. I could see that she had really enjoyed herself, but I had to know.

'Mother, I have never seen you so happy. What happened?'

She turned and looked at me briefly, then turned her attention back to her driving. I had actually done what I dreaded to do. Her face clouded over. Then she said

'I am happy because I have met a man who takes me for who I am...' There was silence after this statement. Then she changed the topic and started asking me how I had enjoyed the party.

I have lost memory of the many things my mother and I talked about that night and later on in our lives. A gate had been opened between us that night. Why did these few words of my mother's imprint themselves so much on my heart, Perhaps, because I felt myself capable of the same thoughts and words? Her statement that evening later in life made me conscious of the twists against which I would have to struggle, the twists I was so sad and astonished to see in my mother. She had created a world of her own, a world in which she maintained her stability. This was in line with her harmonious personality and so it was inconspicuous.

What a lesson to me! My mother could maintain a balance in her life which only a tightrope walker could manage. She kept to the end her desire to care for her family, to be a good wife and mother, always making sacrifices. She did not realize maybe because of her modesty that she could get the best for herself by doing what needed the least effort of will, like the evening of the Njangi Party.

131

Man and Woman

The corridor gave way to an enclosed yard behind. The main building faced the main street and the three others were built behind and they enclosed the yard. At the entrance of the corridor from the main street Celina sat with her head bowed and a loincloth covering her back and shoulders. Any passers-by would have thought that she was outside to enjoy the cool morning air. Mutengene is a very hot town and this heat increases when many people sleep in one room and bodies are too long in close contact.

Celina was not enjoying the cool morning air. She was weeping silently. The two rooms in which Celina and her husband lived faced this central backyard. She did not sit at her door because she did not want anybody to talk to her. She wanted to cry out her frustration without interference.

In spite of her choice of where to wallow in peace in her misery, she could not hide from Mami Kata, the landlady. Mami Kata's main door opened unto the main street. Coming out to enjoy the cool morning air, she saw this figure crouching at the entrance to the corridor. She could not see the face. She wondered who it was, and then she recognised Celina's loincloth. She had not come out with a stool on which to sit and turned round to go back into the house to get one. Before she did she noticed that the shoulders under the cloth were shaking. She stopped and watched. Then she heard a whimpering sound. She moved over to Celina and asked.

'Celina, what are you doing here? Why are you crying?' Before she could finish the question, there was a piercing wail from Celina's room. The baby had woken up and not finding its mother, had started protesting in the way it knew best.

'Celina, the baby is crying. Go and carry her' Celina did not bulge. She pulled the loincloth up and covered her head. She had stopped weeping. This was the position in which she wanted her husband to find her. This was one aspect of the revenge she was meditating.

It was not the first time that she had had to cry out her frustration. She had always done it in their room. She planned it in such a way that he would find her in tears when he came back from work. Each time he found her weeping it sent him raving mad, and this was exactly what she wanted. Often in his rages he threatened sending her away or beating her. She was sure that he was never going to do what he threatened. Whatever he did she knew that he would never send her away or beat her. They would go on like that for ever. That is what made her frantic when her frustrations over took her.

The present situation had started the previous evening when she had told her husband that she wanted a small business of her own. She wanted to make use of the time she spent at home. The street in front of the house was a busy one as men, women and children passed by every day. School children in particular passed along the main street to go to school. If she had a small kiosk she could also sell exercise books, pencils, chalk, biscuits and sweets, in fact all the little things children bought on their way to and from school. She could also sell cigarettes, boxes of matches, magi cube and sugar. These were things that were needed by families on a daily basis. She had even discussed the possibility of putting up a makeshift kiosk at the side of the house with the landlady and she had not been against the idea, but her husband had asked her to wait. He hadn't enough money yet.

That is how he has been asking her to wait for so many things. She had wanted them to move to a better neighbourhood. He had asked her to wait. Before she got pregnant she had wanted to attend evening school. He had asked her to wait. Then she had to wait for the baby to be born. With a two years old baby, evening school was out of the question. Now she had to wait for when there will be enough money before she can start a small business.

But he was a good husband. He provided her with the things she needed which were within his reach. She remembered when she was pregnant with the baby. He had been so excited that he had provided her least fancy. She had been so happy and proud of her husband. She had been taking good care of her baby and husband, but as the months turned into years Celina realised that she could do much more than just care for her baby and husband.

The neighbours were waking up. Mami Kata had gone and taken the baby. She was back in her house attending to the baby. Celina was again left alone at the entrance to the corridor. A neighbour passed by and greeted Celina. She did not answer. She was the occupant of the room next to Celina's.

Because of the heat many of the houses did not have ceilings. Any noise made in one room carried over to the next. He had heard the argument between Celina and her husband and was not surprised to find her weeping outside. Many more tenants were awake and some were going to their marketplaces and some to their jobsites. They passed by Celina and asked no questions nor made any remarks. A woman sitting outside early in the morning weeping was no cause for concern. No family secret could be hidden once the couple allowed their anger to get the better of them. No

135

neighbour intervened in such quarrels unless it erupted into a fight, then they would intervene to safe life. Marital fighting has been known to result in one partner beating the other to death, and most often it is the woman who is beaten to death. Celina did not care whether they pitied or scorned her. It did not mean anything to her at that moment. She wanted the neighbours and even passers-by to know that her husbands had treated her badly. That was what she wanted, at least for now. That was the first part of her programme.

Divine had left for work the previous evening wondering what Celina wanted him to do. He had been angry and frustrated because he thought he was doing his best for her. His work as a nurse at the Mutengene Baptist hospital kept him busy during the day. When he was on night duty he came home exhausted and sleepy.

It was now eight o clock and Celina was still sitting at the entrance of the corridor. She saw a figure approaching. Instinctively she knew it was her husband Divine. Everything in her suddenly went still. Her whole being concentrated with acute intensity, on the sound of the approaching footsteps. She was deaf to all other sounds around her. The steps came nearer. He would soon be near her. She remained motionless, her head resting on her knees. Her eyes closed, waiting.

As soon as Divine saw the figure crouching at the entrance of the corridor he recognised Celina's loincloth and was wondering why she was sitting there. He had completely forgotten about his argument with her. He had been preoccupied with the condition of one of his patients in his ward. He was exhausted. At the age of thirty five he was still consider a young man, but these night shifts wore him out. All he wanted to do that morning was to sleep, but Celina's presence and posture at the entrance to the corridor worried him.

He came and stool near her. With her head bowed she opened her eyes and saw only his toes in his sandals. She did not lift up her head. She closed her eyes and waited.

'What are you doing here?' he asked.

She did not respond. He tried to lift up her head. He saw that she had been weeping. He looked round to see if anybody was watching. Anger took possession of him. Blood drained from his members and the hand that held his bag began to tremble. A feeling of humiliation overwhelmed him. Celina had disgraced him. She wanted everyone, even passers-by; to know that he was a bad husband after all he had done for her. Then he felt weary. His anger drained away. He looked at the silent figure huddled in front of him. What she had done was enough. He did not want any scandal. He repeated softly.

'Why are you crying?' It was as though he was talking to a child. Raising her tear stained blank eyes to him she gazed through and beyond him. Such was the earnestness of that gaze that he turned his eyes away. He dropped his bag and stood looking at her.

'Why are you sitting out here?'

No reply. Her face was again hidden in the folds of her loincloth. So there was no end to it? He thought. At work he had briefly thought about her argument for doing something of her own... and not without blaming himself. What she was asking for was legitimate enough, but he did not want her too... not yet. He held her hand.

'Come let's go'

'The tone with which he spoke this second time was a warning that rage will take control if she did not comply. He kept a firm grip on himself. His raged usually took him beyond him elf.

'Come let's go to the house. You are just behaving like a child.'

The word 'child' made Celina to look up and give him a glance with such ferocity of anger that he shivered. A dispirited sigh escaped his lips.

'What do you want Celina? What do you want me to do?'

He looked at her with an intense gaze as if looking at her that way would produce a solution to the problem. There was no reaction. In a hash tone and almost shouting he said.

'What is the matter with you? Am I not talking to you?'

He hadn't intended to speak so harshly to her, but now it did not matter. He turned from her and started walking into the corridor. He had hardly moved half the length of the corridor when he turned round.

'Celina!' She started, turned round looked at him and bowed her head again without responding.' 'Where is the child?' He walked straight back to her. She could feel his fury as he glared down at her. The child, she had not bothered about the child. Forgetting about the child was part of her revenge too. In her self-absorption she had not thought about the child. She had not foreseen that thinking, that deliberately not thinking about the child would affect her so painfully.

'Where is the child?' he asked again. She thought that he was going to strike her. Even if he had done so, she would not have answered him. It was true that she was using the child as a weapon. Even to her this seemed extraordinary.

'Are you going to answer me or not?' His rage was mounting. He took a deep breath and stepped down from the veranda on which he was standing. He stooped and brought his face to the same level as hers.

'When will you stop behaving as a child and making life difficult for both of us, especially me?'

The agony in his heart came down in his words. Suddenly he remembered how he had suffered when she ran back to her parents in Kumba. He loved her dearly but could not understand why she behaved the way she sometimes did. He put his hand under her chin and lifted her face. She offered no resistance. A feeling of pity flooded him.

'Why do you do this?'

Celina's lips began to tremble. She leaned forward and her face was almost on his shoulders.

'I don't know' She replied. Had he heard well?

'What did you say?'

'Nothing'

Suddenly everything changed.

'Nothing?' he asked. 'Then why? Can you tell me why you are sitting here and weeping? And where is the child?'

Yelling he lifted her to her feet. Passers-by looked at them. They were not fighting. They were not shouting at each other. They just looked like a man helping his wife to get up, but his rage had overwhelmed him and taken over like a fever. He had not expected to be this angry. All along he had kept a firm rein on his anger, but it had slipped out of his hands. This rages and regrets these transitions from pity and tenderness to ferocious anger, how dramatic it all was. How they exhausted him. He had hurt her. Celina stood facing him. She looked into his eyes and said 'Excuse me' Then she walked passed him into the corridor that led to their room

Divine was stunned. He had expected a quarrel or even a fight when he had forcefully held her to stand up. She had

139

ignored him. What was she asking excuse for? He wondered. Maybe she was asking excuse for what she had done or she was just wanted him to let her pass. He concluded on the second, for, there was no sign of remorse on her face.

Mami Kata was standing at the door watching. Celina moved over to her, murmured a thank you and took the baby from her. She went into her room and sat on a chair staring out of the door with a stony look on her face. Divine came in murmuring 'I am tired, tired.'

'Tired? Tied of what?' Celina asked. Her head was splitting with a headache. She wanted all these to end. She had gone too far and was now just rolling in her conflicting emotions like a stone down a hillside. It was as if Divine too had resolved not to speak. Seeing the baby in her arms had calmed him down. Things were not as bad as he had thought. Celina continued.' Tired of what Divine? Tired of me?' Divine did not answer.

'I am waiting for your answer.' She prompted

'Tired of arguing with you.'

'Is that all?' she asked.

'Yes'

'So I am the one who always starts the arguments?'

'No, it is my grandmother.' Then he started laughing. He thought his reply was funny, but he stopped when she lashed out.

'Do you care how I spend my day? You go off to work and your home is well cared for. You come back and eat well cooked food. Do you care?'

Divine was not indifferent to all these. What she did was very important to him Yet...'

'That is no reason why...'

'I know' She sighed.

140

A silence fell between them. It went on and on. It brought certain calm. He had forgotten that he was still standing and holding his bag. He had forgotten too that he was hungry and tired. He was certain that there was no food in the house. Yes, again he had let himself be captured by the deception that he had detached himself from her. He began to talk.

'Celina, I married you because I love you and that love will not change.'

Yes Divine, I know that, but I cannot spend my whole life just doing what I have been doing since I married you.'

Things are going to change Celina. It is not always going to be like this.'

When will that be? You want me to be an old woman before I start thinking of doing something for myself?'

He had not expected Celina to respond. He had thought that as usual she was going to stay quiet and absorb what he was saying. That is what he thought. He thought he was again going to convince her of the sincerity of his words, but her respond changed the flow of his thoughts. Instead he said.

'Don't you see how it all is...so much wasted time? Is life not complicated enough without this? So why do you do it? Just tell me why.'

He came and sat by her side and put his arms around her.

'It's over, isn't it?'

She placed her head on his shoulders and started crying again. She did not know why she was crying. She just felt relieved as she cried. He held her and stroke her back

'Stop crying. It's all over now. I love you Celina. I always will.' She sniffed and wiped her eyes. She wondered what was over. He continued to hold her tenderly and lovingly. She felt calm. It seemed as if her aim was to get him to hold her like that and say those words. Everything else was forgotten completely.

'Divine...'She could not continue. She just held him tight to herself. Divine smiled to himself. He gently stroke her cheek and got up and went into the bedroom. Everything was still in disorder. The bed was unmade. The potty containing the baby's excrement was still there. The window was still shut and the blinds drawn. The room was still full of the smells of the night. He kept his bag on the bedside cupboard. He removed his shirt and hung it on a nail on the wall. Celina walked in and stood by the table on which she kept the box that contained her clothes. Divine waited for her to speak but she said nothing. She passed and sat on the bed, placing the sleeping baby behind her. She held her head in her palms. Divine looked at her.

'You have a headache. I can see.'

'Yes'

'You see how you can make yourself sick over nothing? It is over, isn't it?' He came and got her to stand. Then he took her in his arms and clasped her tenderly. He would have liked not to say anything at that moment. He knew it was better not to say anything just then, yet he began to speak urged by an irresistible impulse.

'Why did you do it?' he asked tenderly. 'Why?'

'And why did you do it?' She asked him.

'I?'

'Yes you. There are two of us. If the fault was only one person's...' She stopped.

'But,' he said. 'No one is at fault.'

'And that is why?'

'What? That things are so?' He asked.

'Yes perhaps'

'Anyhow there is no malice'

'So? She asked eagerly.

'Can you remember what it was all about, because I can't. They were just words and they do not matter'

'So, with all the trouble they have caused? Well forget about it.' She said.

They loosened their arms from around each other. He moved away and sat on the bed.

'I am hungry' Divine said in a flat voice. He did not want to sound accusatory. Celina looked at him and smiled briefly. She moved out of the room and went to the common kitchen outside used by the tenants. Each tenant had a small section where the three stone fireplaces identified the area for each household. She had forgotten to take a box of matches to start the fire with. She went back into the room to get it. The baby had woken up and Divine was carrying her in his arms. He was looking intently at the baby. Without looking up he said.

'Celina, what did I say to you yesterday?'

For a moment she said nothing. Then she said.

'Nothing'

'Nothing?'

'Yes, nothing'

'Yes I said something. Tell me.'

'No, what good will it do?'

'I just want to know

'It is not worth the trouble.' She said

He still waited. Why did she not want to tell him? He wondered. He himself could not remember.

Celina?'

'Yes'.

'Please tell me'

'Why do you want to know? We are not going to start that again. It is so stupid.'

He realized that she was not going to tell him

'All right,' he murmured. 'After all...'

After all it was better that way.

Up To Bamenda

Mbiliensong came up to Bamenda. He came to work for Pa Noubissi in his carpentry workshop. Coming up is an expression that means more than those who use it understand. In the minds of the villagers, going up means a change in the status of the person. The event of going up to Bamenda even for a visit brings much expectation in the heart of the potential visitor and the family concerned.

Going up to Bamenda means enjoying things like entering a taxi to take you wherever you wanted to go, sleeping on a good bed with Dunlop Mattress instead of a bamboo bed, touching something on the wall and the room is flooded with light. It even meant eating rice and stew whenever you wanted because women sold this delicacy in makeshift huts by the roadside.

It meant wearing clean clothes all the time. It meant putting on slippers or shoes all the time. Most important of all it meant looking at lights from the headlamps of cars and street lights in the evening, hearing music from bars all the time and watching people and vehicles as the move up and down the street. It meant listening to what the neighbours were saying without appearing to.

For those who came to Bamenda to stay it meant much more than all of these. It meant looking for and having a job which was not going to the farm every day. It meant you could have money on a regular basis and much more of it even.

Mbiliengsong had completed Class Seven by passing the First School Leaving Certificate but not the Common Entrance Examination into Secondary Schools. He was a big boy in the village and did not see himself going to sit in class with small boys in a college in the town of Ndop. When he had told his father that he did not want to go to college his father was relieved because Mbiliengsong had become so handy in the farm. He could also rely on him to carry out errands for him. He was already fitting into the fabric of village life. He already had his own farm from which he had harvested four bags of groundnuts. This was indicative of the fact that he was a hardworking boy and in the future would be a rich man by village standards if he continued to work hard and increase his farms. His father was already contemplating getting a wife for him although he had not mentioned it to him. His father was foresighted enough to see that if Mbiliensong learnt a trade and established in the village, together with his farms he would be a richer person. Thinking on all these he had decided that Mbiliengsong would go to Bamenda and learn how to make chairs. The growing population in the village and the influx of young people from neighbouring villages coming to exploit the groundnut trade would provide a ready market for him. He had contacted his friend Mr. Noumbissi and the response had been positive.

Mbiliengsong on his part already saw himself as one of the men who in future would be involved in directing the affairs of the village. Living in the village and being part of it, taking part in its traditions and ceremonies prepared one for the propagation and perpetuation of the village's heritage.

When his father had proposed the idea of going to Bamenda to him, he had at first been hesitant. On second thoughts he had realised that this would give him an edge over the other boys who remained in the village. His horizon would be made larger and living in town would increase his image as well. Mbiliengsong before leaving for Bamenda knew what he was going to do but he did not know who he was going to live with. His father had told him that he was going to learn carpentry in his childhood friend's workshop.

His father had gone to primary school at the Native Authority School in Ndop. Both had worked like night watchmen in Bamenda. While he worked as night watchman Mr. Noumbissi had spent his day learning carpentry. He was quiet proficient as a carpenter and did a lot of work in the village but hoped one day to work in town and earn much more money than he was doing in the village. He did not want his skills to be waited in the village.

When Mr. Noumbissi's father died he was made the successor. As the successor in a large family there were many privileges he enjoyed. As successor he had inherited a vast piece of land near the town of Mbouda. He sold off a piece of this land to set up a carpentry workshop at Mile Two Nkwen. He was entitled to a share of the bride price on any of the girls in the large family. His father was not able to open a workshop for him because of the many children he had. But now his dream would become a reality. As successor and being in control of the family wealth he was able to settle comfortably in Bamenda. He now lived in the house his father had built in Bamenda and had put up for rents. Moving to go and live again in Bamenda was not going to be a great transition because as night watchman he had appreciated town life.

Mbiliengsong came to live with Mr. Noumbissi when he was at the height of his business venture. The back yard of the house his father had left for him at Mile Two Nkwen was transformed into a workshop. Part of the front yard had been built up into a display shop.

The evening Mbiliensong arrived from the village Pa Noumbissi was not at home, but he was warmly welcomed. Mrs. Noumbissi, a large woman in her late forties, after looking him over asked Stephanie her house help to take his bag and show him to his room behind the house next to the workshop. When they came back to the sitting room Mrs. Noumbissi was sitting in one of the upholstered chairs that seemed to fill the whole room. Mbiliensong immediately suspected that these were products from her husband's workshop. She filled the chair to the brim. Mbiliengsong stood looking at her. Without looking at him, she asked.

'Stephanie go and get some food for him.' To the boy he said, 'sit down.' Mbiliengsong looked round for a place to seat. The chairs that were near to him were like those on which Mrs. Noumbissi was sitting. He dared not sit down on any one of them. He was about to ask where he should sit when he saw some other chairs arranged round a table. He moved over and sat on one of them. Mrs. Noumbissi smiled to herself. Mbiliengsong did not miss this smile. He sat and waited. Mrs. Noumbissi said nothing neither did she look at the boy.

'What is your name?' She asked out of the silence. Without thinking to give his English name Julius which was simple and easier, he gave the name he was called in the village.

'Mbiliengsong, madam'

'What?'

'My name is Julius Madam.

'No I want the name you first gave.' There was a small smile at the corner of Mrs. Noumbissi's mouth although she had not yet looked at the boy. He realized that he had gotten himself into a tight corner and wanted the easier way out by telling her what she wanted to hear.

'My name is Mbiliensong Madam.'

Mrs. Noumbissi laughed out loud. She lifted up her eyes and looked at the boy. At that moment Stephanie came into the room. Hearing the sound of laughter she thought her madam had called for her.

'Yes madam, you called for me?'

'No Stephanie, I did not call for you. Go back and do your work.' Stephanie did not go. She hid behind the door and listened.

'What does it mean?' Mrs. Noumbissi asked.

'What madam?'

'Your name.'

The boy was trapped. He had never thought of the meaning of his name. He now thought of the meaning of his name in his mother tongue, but how was he to translate it in such a way that it will be understood. Mrs. Noumbissi was still waiting.

'It means 'Outside deny friend'

Mrs. Noumbissi roared with laughter. 'What a funny name. I hope you are going to be as funny as your name'

The boy did not find this funny at all. Stephanie who had been watching and listening behind the door felt drawn to the boy. He was going to be one more of Mrs. Noumbissi's victims, but this was not what was bothering the boy.

Mbiliengsong was determined not to go back to the village. No matter what this woman said or did to him he was going to bear it. And bear it he did with help from Stephanie.

Stephanie was a house help, but she was more the mother of the house than Mrs. Noumbissi. She had babysat three of her children; she went to the market and did the cooking. Her madam relied on her to know what provision was in the house and what was not. She supervised the children when they did their laundry. She understood Mrs. Noumbissi and knew how to get round her.

It was close to six pm, when Mbiliengsong finally left Mrs. Noumbissi sitting room and came behind the house. He did not know where Stephanie had kept food for him. He was really hungry.

'You are going to take a bath first.' Stephanie said as she came out of the kitchen. 'There is water in the bathroom.' She pointed to where the bathroom was next to the kitchen, by the side of the workshop. Mbiliengsong obediently followed her directions. Stephanie brought his food to the room where she had kept his bag and quickly went away. Mbiliengsong after bathing took the food out to the veranda to sit there and eat. It was getting dark and Stephanie came and switched on the safety lights behind the house. Mrs. Noumbissi came behind the house and saw him. The boy did not look at her. Her formidable size and her badmouth scared him, but he was ready for more of what he had received in the sitting room.

'Have you taken a bath? You children from the village have a terrible smell' Mbiliengsong did not answer.

'Who am I speaking to?'

'Yes madam'

'Yes madam, what

'Yes madam Yes.'

Mrs. Noumbissi glared at him and walked away. Stephanie was standing at the kitchen door watching and listening to what was being said. As soon as their madam turned round she ducked into the kitchen. She soon came out. At the sound of her presence at the kitchen door, Mbiliengsong looked up and their eyes met. She smiled and he smiled in turn. His response to their madam had sounded rude, but he could not think of anything else to say. Stephanie had found his response funny. For the first time somebody had had an upper hand on Mrs. Noumbissi. This pleased Stephanie. She saw in Mbiliengsong a boy who could stand up to Mrs. Noumbissi without causing any antagonism. She liked him. She liked the way he looked at her without appearing to. She did not know exactly why but she liked him.

Mr. Noumbissi was a busy and hardworking man. He found in Mbiliengsong a hardworking boy. His raw strength was an added asset. He lifted lengths of planks with such ease. He carried the upholstered chairs that were bought from the show room to the trucks without any help. He never complained about anything. He worked with some inner cheerfulness. Stephanie was very instrumental in this. She acted as a buffer between him and their madam's sharp words by hinting him on her moods, likes and dislikes. She would keep extra food for him. He loved eating rice and Stephanie always kept some for him especially the part that is partly burnt at the bottom of the pot.

Mr. Noumbissi was always in need of planks. He found it lucrative to buy more planks than he needed so that he could sell some to carpenters who engaged in making furniture on a smaller scale or to those constructing houses. He often went out of town to buy planks from neighbouring villages.

Mbiliengsong always accompanied him. Sometimes they stayed as long as one week.

The first time Mbiliengsong went on such a trip Stephanie felt very lonely. She had come to love being with him. She liked his simple ways. There was nothing he could not do to help her. He split wood for her to use in cooking. When there was less work for him in the carpentry workshop he kept her company. When Mrs. Noumbissi was not in the kitchen Mbiliengsong would stand in front the workshop and converse with her. They often threw jokes at each other. Mbiliengsong was grateful that he had found someone with whom he could be himself, someone who did not laugh at his village mentality and ways of doing things.

The wooden shed in which the machines stood was further down the backyard. The kitchen was nearer the main house. The noise from the machine dominated any conversation that was held behind the house. He found time to be with Stephanie. When there was no work to be done especially when the wood work of a set of chairs had been completed and they were waiting for the tailors to cut the cloth and sew them to fit on the Dunlop that had been gummed to the chairs to give them shape, Mbiliengsong would place a chair by the kitchen door and talk with Stephanie as she did her chores in the kitchen. Sometimes he actually went into the kitchen to help her with a bucket of water or just to be near her. He never spent much time in the kitchen because he knew that if Madam met him there, there would be trouble. Stephanie was a kind-hearted girl and used to put more food for the boys than her madam had asked her to. Mrs. Noumbissi would never give that much food to the boys. She considered them all good-for-nothings. To her they were always dirty, noisy and lazy. The boys had developed a technique to outsmart the madam. Each time one of the boys was in the kitchen and Mrs. Noumbissi's footsteps were heard coming to the backyard one of them would whistle. It was becoming evident that Stefanie was paying much more attention to Mbiliengsong that to the other boys. He was the only boy who lived in the compound. The rest of the boys lived in their own places and only came there to work. Mbiliengsong's jovial temperament did not allow any antagonism to develop especially when they commented about his special relationship with her.

Mr. Noumbissi' trips in search of planks took him further afield. Much more planks were coming from the village of Befang in Wum in Menchum Division. Mr. Noumbissi wanted to exploit this new source by going there himself and making contacts with suppliers in the village and giving them money in advance so that a good quantity of planks would be reserved for him. This was a lucrative way of buying planks, for when the prices were increased, the people who had taken money from him would be stuck with the prices agreed upon. Apart from selling to people in town he had captured the market and was even selling to people who came to Befang to buy planks. Transporting the planks from the remote places where the trees were found was a problem many of the other buyers did not want to face.

On one of his trips to Befang Mbiliengsong had accompanied him. He had made Befang a sort of collection point, for the planks now came from as far as the villages of Esu and Weh. Miliengsong had to go to these villages to supervise the packing and transportation of the planks. During the day his work kept him busy, but during the night he wished he were in town. The dark nights, the heat and the mosquitoes kept him uncomfortable. It was just like being in the village, but he was consoled by the fact that he would soon be going back to town. He missed Stephanie.

Stephanie missed him too. She missed his smile and the jokes they shared together in the evenings. She missed the stories he told her about his village. She enjoyed the stories because the events were just like that of her own village. Sometimes she told him stories about her own village, but hers were not as interesting as the ones he told her. Mbiliengsong loved his job, but his long stay in Esu was making him weary. He missed Stephanie. He missed the extra helpings of rice and stew which she usually kept for him. He loved eating rice. He missed her teasing. He missed her laughter.

Mbiliengsong arrived with the first truck of planks on a Sunday morning at 10 am. They had left Befang at 4am. They offloaded the truck and after bathing and eating he went to sleep. He was tired but happy. He had made a lot of money on this trip. He had kept some of the money he was to use in paying the boys who loaded the trucks because he had done the work himself. He had bought a present for Stephanie. He did not know whether she was going to like it, but that was not his problem for now. All he wanted to do was to sleep.

Mbiliengsong got up at five pm that evening. He put on the light in his room and waited. He thought that Stephanie would see the light in his room and come to greet him, but she did not come. He went outside and looked at her door. It was closed and dark. Mbiliengsong had a sinking sensation of disappointment. There was nothing for him to do that evening. He had slept for the most part of the day and sleep would elude him for most of the night. He strolled to the front of the hose and walked to the roadside. Before leaving the village his father had warned him about the evils in town.

He had warned him about the easy ways of getting money and the easy ways of spending it. He had warned him particularly against alcohol and women. For ten months in town he had kept to his father's advice. As Mbiliengsong stood and watched people and vehicles going up and down, someone tapped him on the shoulders.

'Rambo!' He turned. One of the boys, Jack who had come back with them from Befang that morning, was looking at him and smiling. Mbiliengsong had been nicknamed Rambo because of his raw strength. The boy continued. 'What are you doing standing by the roadside?'

'I am just enjoying the evening air and watching people and vehicles pass by.'

'Is this the best way for you to enjoy yourself?'

Mbiliengsong did not answer. He did not know what to say and thought his silence would be understood, but Jack did not understand.

'There are better ways of enjoying the evening. For the past week you have been working so hard. It is good that you relax in a better way. In fact I have never seen you out in the evening. Are you a rat mole always hiding in your hole?' Mbiliengsong was offended but he hid his annoyance. He was good at doing this.

'What do you mean? Am I not outside now?'

Jack was defeated. He had a mission to achieve. He had been sent by the other boys to come and look for him. If Jack had not met him at the roadside he would have come to his room.

'Well, I just wanted you to enjoy yourself with other people, not alone. Come and see.'

Mbiliengsong followed him. They moved up the street to Mile Two Junction. Jack led him to an on-licence bar. There were chairs and tables outside. Once there, Jack steered him to a table where some boys were sitting. At first Mbiliengsong could not identify the occupants because of the dim lights. When he got nearer a shout welcomed him.

'Rambo! Rambo!' Mbiliengsong knew all the three boys who were sitting there. They were all apprentices who had often come to Mr. Noumbissi's workshop to have their planks cut and shaped. Mbiliengsong smiled. He liked the way his strength was appreciated. Jack went into the bar and brought out another chair for him. He sat down. Jack went into the bar again and came out with a bottle of Mitzig beer and placed it in front of him. Mbiliengsong looked at the boys. Each of them had a bottle of Mitzig in front of him which was half full. Jack opened the bottle without asking his opinion.

'Hey! Wait.' Mbiliengsong protested. 'Why did you open the beer without asking whether I was going to drink it?'

'You have been out of town for one week. You have worked very hard. You need to relax. Nothing relaxes a person like a bottle of Mitzig.' The other boys were looking at him smiling and affirming what Jack was saying. He could see that they were all relaxed and enjoying themselves. Mike encouraged him.

'This is very mild beer. It is not going to worry you.'

'That is not what I meant.' Mbiliengsong replied. He did not want the image he had created in the minds of those boys to be tarnished by a bottle of beer. He continued.' In the village the palm wine we drink is stronger than this.' As he spoke he indicated the bottle with a bit of disdain. To pierce Mbiliengsong's shell further jack said.

'If you do not have money for the beer we will pay for you' He got the desired effect.

'Money is not the problem. It is just that...' Mbiliengsong had never drank beer before, but he did not want his friends to know this. '...it is just that I do not like Mitzig, but since it has been opened, I will drink it.'

'Now you are talking', Solomon, one of the boys remarked. 'I thought you were going to reject our offer'

After taking a deep breath Mbiliengsong lifted the bottle to his mouth and took a sip. It tasted a bit bitter but he swallowed it. After some time he took another seep. The boys were looking at him.

'How does it taste?' Jack asked.

'It is not bad.'

'You see, I told you that Mitzig is the best beer.'

As they drank Jack told the boys how Mbiliengsong carried heavy lengths of wet plank as if they were just pieces of dry wood. The reactions and responses of the boys made Mbiliengsong proud of himself. He could not stop Jack from exaggerating in his narration. It all added to the fun of the evening. By now Mbiliengsong's bottle was almost empty. He began to feel great though he did not speak much. He now liked the taste and the feel of the beer as it slid down his throat. He slowed down on his drinking. He did not know what was going to happen next and he did not know how he was going to react if he was offered another bottle of beer. His companions had finished theirs and had gotten other bottles.

'Your beer will go flat. You are not even drinking' One of the boys remarked. Mbiliengsong felt funny. His stomach churned and he felt hot. He had not eaten that evening but he ignored this fact and emptied the bottle. He wanted to go home but he did not know how he was going to extricate himself from these boys. What excuse was he going to give?

He knew that whatever excuse he gave was going to be brushed aside by these boys and he did not want to be seen as a chicken hearted boy who could not hold two bottles of beer in his stomach. Jack got up and went into the bar for another bottle for him.

Mbiliengsong watched and listened as the boys talked. They did not seem to be affected by the beer. Jack placed the bottle of beer in front of him. He did not want to disappoint himself. He was not different from these boys and he was not going to allow himself to be different. He pushed the empty bottle aside. He was about to lift the second bottle to his lips when his father's voice rang with such clarity in his ears that he thought he was behind him. He turned round to look. The voice said 'Beware of beer and women, they bore holes in your pockets.' Mbiliengsong stalled. He did not know whether to stop or to continue. Then he threw caution to the winds. How careful was he going to be? He was no longer in the village and had to learn a bit of what the town had to offer. In doing this he assured himself that he would never allow himself to get drunk. If he succeeded in drinking the second bottle then he would never try again. This evening was going to be the first and the last. With this conviction he lifted the bottle to his lips and took a sip.

It was eleven thirty pm when Mbiliengsong got back to his room. His head was aching, his stomach was churning and his eyes were heavy. He saw the light shining in Stephanie's room. His head cleared a bit and he remembered the gift he had bought for her. The purse was hidden in the bag where he kept his best pair of trousers and shirt. This was the best time to give her, but he was hungry. He had never gone to Stephanie's room so late in the night, but he had an excuse.

She had not given him his supper. He went over and knocked at her door.

'Stephanie, Stephanie, are you awake?'

There was silence in the room and he was afraid that she might be deep asleep and his insistent knocking might alert the occupants of the main house. He did not want his absence to be known. Stephanie opened the door.

'Where have you been? I came back and knocked at your door but there was no answer.'

'I went out.'

With who?' Mbiliengsong could not lie. He did not even see the need for it, so he told her what had happened that evening. He continued.

'I am hungry, is there food for me?'

'Have I become your wife for you to get me up in the night asking for food? If you do not promise to give me something in return I am not going to give you food.' Mbiliengsong was not surprised at what she had said, for she had always said so and given him what he wanted without his giving her anything. But this evening was different. He had something for her but did not want to reveal it so soon.

'How can you treat me this way Stephanie? You are my cherie coco, you know that.'

'What Cheirie coco? You came back since morning and you did not bother where I had gone to.'

'How could I have found out? When I came back I did not see you. Madam told me that my food was in the kitchen. I went and took it but I could not ask her where you were. Just give me the food and see what I am going to do.'

'What are you going to do? Have you ever done anything for me in spite of all I do for you?'

'Just give me the food and see what I am going to do.'

She went to the kitchen took his flask of food and came and kept it at his door and turned to go away. Mbiliengsong had gone to his room and taken out the purse. When he heard her keep the flask he called.

'Stephanie come in.' when he received no answer he came out of his room and saw Stephanie standing outside.

'If you have something for me give me out here. I am not coming into your room.'

'Okay come to the workshop. I do not want us to stand outside here. That is patron's window. He might get up at the sound of our voices.' He held her hand and led her to the workshop. Stephanie obeyed without question. She was too excited to see what Mbi had to give her. His name was to long for her and she had shortened it to Mbi which sounded more intimate. She was excited too at the way he was behaving. He was holding her hand and the way he looked at her was different. She had waited for just such a reaction from him. She followed him passed the kitchen into the workshop. This was where the machines that smoothed the planks and got them into various shapes were housed. There was wood shavings and saw dust on the floor. Mbiliengsong held her hand, pushed the door open slowly and led her into the workshop. His eyes were shining and his heart was thumping. He looked at her, and then he clasped her hands and put the purse between her palms. Stephanie held the purse and moved nearer to the doorway where the light from the single naked bulb that hung there shone better. Mbiliengsong was left in the dark. He saw the smile spread over her face. He felt happy that he had thought of getting a present for her. She turned and looked at him. He was in the dark and she was in the light. The smile on her lips made her face look radiant. He felt happy to be the cause of such a smile. Stephanie looked towards the main house to make sure that no one was watching or coming. Then she moved into the dark and put her arms round Mbiliengsong's neck. He held her close. His heart was thumbing and he was afraid that she might feel it. He tried to prevent this by pushing her away gently, but she thought that he was just adjusting himself and held him closer. He could feel her body trembling. He did not know what to do or say, or what was going to happen next. He wanted to tell her that they should stop, but his throat was dry and his mouth could not form any words. Stephanie was saying

'Oh thank you. Thank you so much. You are such a good and nice boy'

The mixture of hunger and dizziness was weighing him down and he moved to the wall to support himself. Stephanie thought this move was to give them more stability so she clung to him.

The solution to his present predicament was to play along with her, but he was hungry and could not play along with hunger.

'Stephanie I am hungry. Since I ate in the morning I have not eaten again.'

'Don't you like me, Mbi?'

'I have not said I do not like you. I like you that is why I bought this purse for you.'

'Don't you like it when I hold you?' To this he could not respond. He liked her holding him but he knew what this could lead to and he did not want it, not now when he was in this state.

'I like it, but I am tired. Do you like the purse?' He changed the topic of conversation

'I like it very much. It is very nice. Mbi I like you very much and will give you all you want'

At the last statement his head cleared a bit. He looked at Stephanie. He did not want to believe what she was saying. He had thought she was just playing up to him. His body was telling him something but his stomach over ruled.

'Thank you Stephanie for the food. I will see you tomorrow' He extricated himself from her and mover outside. Stephanie followed clutching the purse in her hand. She could not understand Mbi's reaction. She had been certain that he was going to go all the way. She knew that it was the man who asked the women, but Mbi had not asked her. She was just trying to help him along, but he had behaved in a very strange way. Back in her room she was worried about how she was going to react to Mbi in the morning. What if his reaction meant that he did not like her? What was she going to do? What if Mbi ignored her the next day and the days to come? She was smart to know that he would not do such a thing. It would be a dead giveaway. If he did then she would just have to pretend that nothing had happened and leave all the explanation on his plate.

While Stephanie lay thinking of all these possibilities Mbi had eaten his food and before falling into a deep sleep had told himself that tomorrow was another day to be handled as it came, but concerning Stephanie he just had to do soothing about her. He could not ignore what had happened between them that evening. In one night he had been exposed to what his father had warned him about, but he was going to handle them in his own way.

The Cost of Winning

I knew that my husband had another wife. He told me so when we got really serious, but from what he told me I believed that she was not going to be a problem. She was a mission teacher way of in Ndu in the Donga and Mantung Division of the North West Province of Cameroon. My husband made me to understand that he could only work in the Ministry in Yaounde. Since the other woman was not ready to come to Yaounde, I felt secured.

The four years I spent with Sammy in Yaounde was one long honey moon.

I met Sammy at a seminar that lasted for one week. I was one of the participants at this seminar which was organized to train some health personnel as animators for the fight against HIV/AIDS. In addition to this the health personnel came in contact with patients on a daily basis and it was important that they should be knowledgeable on its modes of transmission, prevention and helping patients to learn to live with the virus. Their main job was to sensitize the population on the existence of the virus.

Many communities still looked on any information on the virus with suspicion. Some believed the whole scenario of HIV/AIDS was the creation of Western Powers to prevent the population of Africa from increasing. They felt threatened by the rate of immigrants from Africa to Europe and America. Some believed that it was witchcraft that had been given another name. Those who were infected refused to acknowledge the fact and went to traditional doctors who promise them instant cure, instead of going for medical advice. It was necessary and even urgent for the people to be educated on the actual existence of the virus, its modes of transmission, its symptoms, its prevention and help that can be given to those infected and affected.

Sammy was one of the resource persons. He gave his talk on the second day. His talk was based on the effects of the virus on the human immune system. He spoke with ease, his words flowing out with vitality and confidence.

The information he was giving out was very technical. He used slides, charts and pictures to drive home the information he was giving out. The hall was quiet as the participants listened attentively and took down notes. I could not take my eyes off his captivating personality. Much of the time I did not quite get what he was saying because I was busy admiring the way he spoke and moved about the stage. His suit was well cut and fitted his tall slim body. His finger nails were well trimmed and neat. I looked at his middle finger and remembered what some of my friends had told me about a man's middle finger. It was long and shapely I wondered whether it would be the right size for me. He had a manner of pocketing his left hand while he gesticulated with his right hand as he sauntered up and down the stage. My eyes were glued to his face; my ears heard what he was saying but my mind was elsewhere.

The seminar participants were given lunch and supper but they were not lodged. During lunch and supper the first day he did not appear for lunch and supper at the refectory of the School of Post and Telecommunication where the seminar was taking place. I looked round for him wondering where he must have gone to. I wanted to get to know him and was disappointed.

On the third day he did not come at all. I kept hoping that he would come, but he did not. I believed that since he had given his talk he will not come again until the closing day of the seminar when both resource persons and participants were expected to be present, but that would be too late.

On the fourth day he did not come. I pushed thoughts of him to the back of my mind and concentrated on the lectures and workshops.

The fifth day was a busy one. We visited a number of laboratories in town. We were shown how far these laboratories had been equipped for the screening and testing of the HIV/ AIDS. A demonstration on HIV testing was carried out in one of these laboratories following the ELISA method. We watched a documentary on pre and post testing counselling.

By evening we were exhausted. I was one of the last persons to be seated for supper that evening. I could have gone home immediately after the work of the day but I did not want to face the added task of preparing supper for myself so I stayed for supper. I sat on a table near the door. There were just two people seated there. As the days of the seminar decreased so was the number of people who came for supper. We were waiting for our turn to go to the table to serve ourselves when Sammy walked in, spotted an empty seat on our table and moved over. He kept his car keys and dairy on the table before sitting down. I felt my heartbeat accelerating. I was so excited that I hid my face with my palms, pretending to be bore.

'Hey, what is wrong with you?' Sammy asked trying to pull my hand away from my face. One of the men on the table came to my rescue.

'She must be tired. We have done a lot of movement around today. Sir, you have been missing these last days.'

Their attention was diverted from me and I was grateful. I took off my hand from my face and concentrated on watching the queue as it progressed towards the table laden with food. The three men continued to chat after Sammy had briefed them on what had kept him away. The men had the type of respect for Sammy which can only be found between a teacher and his former students who happen to be working in the same field.

We were soon on the queue along with the others. Once back to our seats we ate in silence. It was the type of silence that exists among strangers who due to circumstances have to eat together but the silence on my part was brittle. It was soon broken by Sammy who between mouthfuls asked one of the men where he worked. The conversation started flowing as we ate. I do not know how Sammy managed it but he soon had all of us talking and even laughing. In the course of the conversation I let them know where I worked and my home origin. It is not normal in such situations for introductions to be made but they sort of just came out in the course of the conversation. Sammy indirectly asked for more information about me which I just laughed off.

Mr. Sammy Zabo gave us a lift on our way home. The two men lived in the Melen neighbourhood while I lived in Biyamassi. He decided to take the road through Carrefour EMIA. He dropped the two men at the Melen Market and that was the beginning of our four year honeymoon.

When I think of those four years, I can do anything to put back the clock. Sammy was all a woman could want of a man. He had told me that he was married but by then I had gone too far to sanely separate from him. Six months later we signed our marriage in court. His marriage certificate with his first wife had the status of polygamy, so there was not much ado. Every minute spent with Sammy was a heaven on earth. 'Betty my love, honey, my darling' were the endearments he poured into my ears daily. His actions matched his words. He was so loving and understanding. I thanked my stars for having attended that seminar. Although I often heard stories that I had taken some other woman's husband- the word was 'husband snatcher' the relevance of their insinuation did not bother me because Sammy often went to Bamenda on mission. Ndu is his home town and he has a house there in which his first wife and children lived, so I could not deceive myself that he did not visit them. I did not allow this knowledge to cloud the bright skies of our love for each other. We never allow her existence to come between us. I earned a reasonable salary and helped him when I could without seeming to bribe him to love me.

The height of our bliss was when we were expecting our first baby. Sammy indulged my every whim. In the excitement of being pregnant I indulged myself with eating and gained weight as the baby grew in my stomach. Sammy was all attention. We could spend hours sitting in the parlour watching TV while he cradled me in his arms, patting my stomach from time to time. He often said that I was a blessing to him and the greatest gift he had ever had was the baby in my stomach. I often wondered whether he had felt the same way when his first wife was pregnant with the two children they had. I did not allow such thoughts to linger in my mind because what was important was the present not the past.

The baby was born and we continued in this bliss. I soon regained my slim figure and Sammy was delighted. He had once told me that what had attracted him to me was my slim straight figure and the way I walked and during my pregnancy he was afraid that I was going to lose my shape. I was surprised that I was able to breastfeed my baby until the age of ten months. We are both of the medical field and know the importance of breast feeding so I was not ashamed to do this. This was also important as it kept my menstrual cycle from coming into action until six months after delivery. From the way we could not keep away from each other I could have gotten pregnant within months of giving birth. I thanked God for giving me such a system which I am sure I inherited from my mother.

I was in the early months of my second pregnancy when the bomb fell. Sammy was appointed as Provincial Coordinator for the fight against HIV/AIDS in the North West Province. The ministry had launched a nationwide campaign and someone had to coordinate the activities in this province. When I hear the announcement I was agitated. His new position did not interest me. I had a feeling that there was going to be trouble, for I immediately recognised the significance of this appointment. For the first time since I met Sammy I felt really sad. I waited anxiously for Sammy to come home for me to see how he was taking this appointment. Sammy was excited and happy about it but my response when he broke the news to me slightly dampened his excitement.

'Hey my angel, are you not happy for me? You know what this means. It is going to change our lives. We are no longer going to live in a small cramped house like this.'

'Yes it is going to change our lives. Nothing will ever be the same again.'

'What do you mean by that?'

I looked at him steadily in the eyes. He seemed to have understood what I meant but did not allow it to cloud his happiness.

'Ma Belle, nothing is going to change. You will see'

'Sammy don't you realize that we are going to Bamenda. Don't you realise what that means?'

'Yes I do. But as I say, nothing is going to change. You will see.

I wanted to believe him but something kept nagging in my mind. I felt uncomfortable with the whole situation, but I had to be cheerful for Sammy's sake. Although he made as if a change of scene would be good for us, I could sense the strain of the implications of the transfer on him. We had settled into a comfortable routine of living and loving. We had made sincere and valuable friends. Living in the capital city had its advantages. One had important information first hand and strings could be pulled in various ministries with ease. I had thought that I was comfortably married and settled and had invested my savings into a hair dressing salon business which was paying well. Now all of these had to be left behind. As if in reaction to the situation little Liza cried and fretted unnecessarily. I had to keep a firm reign on my temper not let it go off. The following week we stated making plans for moving to Bamenda but events overtook us. Sammy had to go to Bamenda and start work immediately. The authorities were in a frenzy to reach as many people and as fast as possible with every available information on HIV/AIDS.

Left alone in Yaoundé I fretted and worried. I worried about everything, but what I worried about most was the fact that it would be easier now for my mate to join us. I had accepted to be second wife without thinking of the possibility of sharing Sammy with another woman. It was now a reality and I tried to be positive about it because before marrying Sammy I knew that he had another woman. I repeatedly assured myself that I was going to take it easy and live my life in spite of her. I prayed for the courage to accommodate the other woman in our lives, but it was not going to be easy.

After two weeks in Bamenda, Sammy paid me a weekend visit. He was all enthusiasm. He talked about the type of life people lived in Bamenda. Food was cheap, house rents were low, house help was easy to get and people were friendly and hospitable. He was more concerned with the physical benefits. He did not think about the emotional complications

A month later Sammy phoned to tell me that he had gotten a five bedroom house in the Azire neighbourhood in Bamenda. The present occupant, a medical doctor had been transferred to Buea and will soon be leaving the house. He ended the call that all was going to be fine. He added the famous dictum 'Love conquers all'

Sammy came for us a month later. He arrived on a Friday night and we had to move on Sunday morning. We had to sell our set of chairs because as he said there were better ones in Bamenda at affordable prizes. A truck carried our luggage while we travelled in the car.

We arrived in Bamenda at four o clock in the afternoon. There were boys ready to off load the entire luggage. I supervised where each item was to go. I was so excited to have so much space to myself. After the cramped rooms we had occupied in Yaounde for the first time this move looked like a blessing, but it was hell in disguise. Within two months I was comfortably settled in my new home. I had a new baby sitter to look after little Liza. There was not much change in my relationship with my husband. Sammy was his usual self and we picked up the thread of our lives.

I was into the fifth month of my pregnancy and was due another visit to my gynaecologist in Yaounde. Two days before I left for Yaounde, in a very casual manner Sammy told me that his first wife might be joining us soon. Since our arrival in Bamenda he had never mentioned the fact, so I did not take him seriously. I was more preoccupied with my health and left for Yaounde.

I left on a Sunday. I made the mistake of not finding out whether the doctor was in town before travelling. When I got to Yaounde I was informed that the doctor had gone to Douala and would be back by in three days. I had to wait for him. I preferred to wait than to go back to Bamenda and come back again. I stayed with one of our closest family friends, Mr. And Mrs. Labane. They were the couple that made me want to be married and when I married Sammy I wanted my marriage to be like theirs. When I told Mrs. Labane what Sammy had said about his second wife coming to live with us, I momentarily saw alarm in her face, and then she laughed and said that Sammy was not serious. She went on to give all the reasons why she thought that Sammy could not do such a thing. She was wrong. She was not Sammy. While waiting for the doctor I did some shopping for myself and the baby. I did not forget Sammy. I loved giving him gifts because of the way he received them.

When I came back from Yaounde I found my mate already occupying the two rooms that had been left vacant. I was so shocked that I could not say anything. That evening I behaved as if nothing had happened and waited for Sammy to come back. Even when he came back I did not say anything. He watched me that evening trying to read into my eyes. I avoided eye contact with him. Later in bed he held me close, kissing the nape of my neck and caressing my protruded stomach. I had my back turned to him. I did not want him to kiss me on the lips. I had always enjoyed his kisses and caresses but that night I lay like a stone. He soon could not bear my silence and lack of response.

'Betty, why are you pretending?'

I gave leash to the anger and tension boiling in me.

'Pretending about what? Pretending that I do not feel you touching me or that your other wife is not in the house?'

The venom with which I said this coupled with my moving out of his arms rendered him speechless. This had never happened between us and I did not know what to do or say next or what to expect. I lay quiet waiting to see what he was going to do.

'What have I done Betty?'

The question made me angrier.

'You lied to me Sammy.' I lashed back and started weeping.

'What did I lie about Betty? You knew that I had a wife but you loved me enough to accept the fact by marrying me. Will her presence change your love for me?'

'I do not Know Sammy, I do not know.' I sobbed.

This time when he moved nearer me and sent his arms round me I did not resist. Then he tried to make me understand and accept the situation

'Betty, do you think that I brought her here to make you miserable? I cannot do such a thing if I had a choice.

'Yes Sammy you had a choice. All these years she has lived without you and you without her and none of you have died.'

'I could have died if I did not meet you Betty.'

'How did I save you?

'With your beauty, your love and your understanding'

I knew where he was drifting to. He had often used this approach to express how he felt for me and to disarm me. Whenever anything annoyed me he smoothened it out this way, but this was not a simple annoyance.

'You are the man. You should have taken a decision'

'You cannot understand Betty'

'Yes I cannot understand because I am so dull.'

Sammy was getting exasperated

'Betty, why are you doing this to me? Why are you being so difficult? It is a simple situation.

'How simple is it? Tell me Sammy. You bring your other wife in the house without telling me and you say that it is a simple thing?

'But I told you before you went to Yaounde

'Yes you did but you were so casual that I thought you were joking. Sammy where are we heading to? This appointment has done more harm than good. I do not know how we are going to cope with this type of situation.

'Betty, listen to what I am going to tell you, and please do believe me. Left to me she would not have come here. I tried to convince her to remain in Ndu to no avail. She even got my parents to her side. The last time I went to the village it was all hell. My parents even told me not to visit them again if she is left in Ndu. What was I to do? For our sakes Betty, do not make our lives unbearable.

We were lying together that night and I wondered whether there will not be nights when by obligation he would have to sleep in the other woman's room. I prepared myself for any eventuality.

It was easier to wait and see what was going to happen, but the practicalities of living from day to day under the present condition were not easy. I had occupied the main kitchen and there was no way she could come in there. I was afraid that she was going to insist on using the kitchen, but she did not. I was grateful for that. We were used to eating together as a family, but now it was impossible. I could not bring myself to make friendly overtures towards her, neither did she. She cooked on a table cooker she had installed in one of the rooms. During the first week I served food for Sammy on the dining table and we ate together. At this time my mate would remain in her room and warn her two children not to come out. Sammy was not comfortable with this. All her actions indicated that she was determined to ignore my presence and I was ready to ignore hers too.

How could we even say good morning to each other when we both had grievances towards the other? We were like two angry lions separated by a very thin wall. I could not imagine how long this was going to last. Sammy did everything to get the two of us together. The first time he called the two of us to talk over the situation with him was a failure. We both sat quiet and gave no answer or response to Sammy's questions and suggestions. Actually, I had nothing to say. I was dying to hear what the other women would say, but she said nothing. Sammy said his piece about the necessity of peace in the family and he was relying on the two of us to examine ourselves and make up our differences. He concluded by saying that his love was not going to change. When he said this I looked at him straight in the eyes. He looked at me too in the eyes .I wondered whether the other women saw this exchange. I also wondered whether the statement was meant for the two of us or only to me. When I looked at her, her gaze was focused on the table in front of her. I could have given everything to know what was going on in her mind at that moment.

Sammy had become used to spending some time with the other woman and occasionally ate there. Each time he did that he also ate what I had kept for him. I knew that this was only a way to sober me up. Then he started sleeping in the other woman's room.

The first time he did this I heard his car drive into the garage. Soon I heard voices in the other section. I could not sleep. I waited for him to come to my room or go to his, but he did not. At five o clock in the morning I heard him go to his room. Soon after there, was a knock at my bedroom door. I knew that he was the one and I did not want to open the door. Then I thought that it would be childish not to. I got up and opened the door. I was boiling with anger and did not know how to react to his presence. He moved straight to the bed and climbed into the sheets. I went to the other side of the bed and also climbed in making sure that I stayed as far away from him as possible. We slept in silence and at seven o clock in the morning he got up and went into his room without saying anything. I did not get out of bed. I did not prepare any breakfast for him. I expected my mate to prepare his breakfast but she did not. When Sammy was ready for work he came to the table and on seeing nothing there called for the two of us.

'Why is there no breakfast for me"? Sammy asked. There was no response. 'What have I done to the two of you that you want to starve me? Have I committed a crime by marrying two wives?' Getting no response he turned and walked to the door. He stopped, turned and looked at me. He wanted to say something but could not. He looked at me for some time, turned round and walked to the door and banged it as he walked out. My mate also turned and walked into her room. I stood alone in the parlour and looked at myself in the mirror of Sammy's eyes.

I told myself to take it easy and give the other woman the chance to take care of Sammy. Many of his clothes were in the wardrobe in my room and he took his bath in the bathroom of the master's bedroom which I occupied. He had moved out to occupy another room as he said not to appear discriminatory. His shirts became dirty and I did not touch them. He soaked his underpants in detergent in a bucket in the bathroom and they remained there for days. Sammy would complain to no one in particular how he could not get a clean shirt to wear. He had been used to meeting his clothes clean and pressed. I stopped taking his coats to the cleaners. The other women had to do her own share of the work.

Tension was mounting higher and higher. My mate was more at ease. She even came into the kitchen where I cooked to take things. This did not bother me, but her attitude when we met along the corridor or behind the house got on my nerves. She would look at me with a condescending smile on her face and make provocative noises.

One day I made a mistake which I regretted later. I threw comments at no one in particular but aimed at her.

'Some people can only feed from what falls off my plate.'

'Oho, she responded. Some people are already starving what have they seen? More is to come.'

This touched me because for some days now Sammy had not come to my room. After this incident we used every opportunity to nip and jibe at each other.

Then the situation became unbearable. Mt thoughts kept me awake and restless most nights. I lost appetite. My next visit to the prenatal clinic at the Bamenda Provincial hospital showed that I had lost weight and my haemoglobin level was lower.

Sammy too was bearing the brunt of the situation. He looked stressed, unhappy and haggard. His shirts were becoming discoloured at the armpits. The shirts and coats he wore to work were creased. More often now I heard their voices raised against each other when he went to my mate's room. When he came to mine he received sullen silence. I felt sorry and started preparing food for him. I kept it on the table in the dining room but did not sit there to eat with him. On some days he ate and on others he did not. I did not mind. Occasionally my mate also kept him food on the table.

It was a ridiculous situation. Although it was stressful I also found it funny. Sammy blew off one afternoon when he came back from work and there was no food for him. I had just come back from the market and had not started cooking. I believed that my mate had kept food for him. Soon after she too came in, so we were both present to watch Sammy break down.

'What is the use of marrying two women if you cannot even have food to eat? I had told you people to settle your differences, but you both are too proud and headstrong to listen to me. My clothes are left dirty; I eat in my own house as if I am eating in a restaurant. I am a stranger in my own house. Yet I have two educated wives. One calls herself a teacher. Is that what you teach your children? And the other...'

Both of us were standing at our respective doors watching him. Sammy stopped turned around and looked at me. He could into continue. He looked at me for some time and walked into his room banging the door behind him. My mate also turned and went into her room. I stood alone in the parlour and looked at myself in the mirror of Sammy's accusations. I was a failure. I had failed myself. I had not kept to my promise of being happy no matter the situation. I was not taking it easy and was not living my life as I wanted to. I was living the type of life my mate wanted me to live. I asked myself if I could not live happily with Sammy even with her around. I saw a possibility in the question but it all depended on Sammy.

In my jealousy I did not notice that I was helping to destroy myself as well as Sammy. He was no longer the man I used to know. In addition to this I was missing him terribly. I wanted him to be with me. I wanted life to be what it used to be. I wanted to retrieve what I had lost. I had to make sacrifices. Making sacrifices meant I had to be tolerant and make the best out of the situation.

I walked towards Sammy's bedroom. I knocked on the door and he opened it as if he was waiting. I entered and we stood and looked at each other. During those few seconds, much of the past was seen in our mind's eyes. Then we embraced. Sammy held me tight but the embrace could not be complete because of my stomach.

'I am sorry Sammy. I am really sorry' I murmured in his ears.

'It's alright Betty. It's unfortunate that things are happening this way. It has not been easy, I know. And it is not going to be easy, but please do try. I know the type of woman you are. If you try things will work out'

'But you have to try too Sammy. Much more important is the fact of the necessity of your presence here. Do not be a victim of what you have come to Bamenda to fight against. I hope you understand what I am talking about.'

'Betty It has not come to that'

'Will it'? Well, if it has to be, then you know what to do.' I had to make Sammy know that in spite of my mate's presence I still loved him and cherished our relationship but he had to do something about her HIV status, for one never knows. I knew this was another area of contention I was raising. I had to because it was a necessity. Both of us had done our HIV screening before we signed our marriage. Then I changed the topic.

'You know that I cannot do all the work. She has to do her own share. She is your wife too.'

'Yes I know, but if she wants me to suffer, will you also do so?'

I could not answer. All I wanted was to be a happy woman in spite of my mate.

'There is something I cannot understand Sammy'

'What is it?'

'After all these years...'

'I go there for the sake of the children. I cannot pretend that I am not their father"

Sammy had read my mind. I wanted to believe him but thought otherwise in order not to be hurt.

When my transfer came through, I started work. Being out of the house, helped a lot. I had to do everything to maintain peace between Sammy and myself without antagonizing anybody. I remembered some of the things I used to do when we were in Yaounde. I took his suits and shirts and trousers to the cleaners. I made sure that his under wears were clean. I packed his bag when he had to travel. I prepared his most cherished dish, fufu corn and huckleberry with roasted chicken called 'Kati Kati' every Sunday

Whenever he came to my room I made sure that we sat and talked. This relaxed him. The parlour was no man's land. We never spoke about the other woman. We both acknowledged that she was a fixture in our lives. We talked mostly about work and the baby soon to be born. We talked about little Lisa and the nursery school she would go to. We reminisced about our lives in Yaounde. Whenever he ate in the other woman's room or spent the night away from my room, I assured myself that it was inevitable. I tried to make myself understand that she too needed attention. It was not an easy thing to do, but I tried. I took it as a duty to make Sammy happy. In the process I was making myself happy too, but I could not fit my mate in the picture.

The Dust of Graffiland

'**D**id you wash the white shirt you wore to church on Sunday? You know that form three is a higher class and you have to spend more time reading your books'

'I did not wash it.'

'Why?'

'It will only get dirtier'

'If you wash it?'

'Yes'

'Mami Milia could not ask how this could be because of the heavy bag she was carrying. The muscles on her neck were paining. She lifted up the bag to release the strain on her neck muscles and asked.

'What do you mean? How can you wash your shirt and it becomes dirty?'

Lientueh did not want to answer. He was carrying his travelling bag filled with his clothes, little bags of parched and unparched groundnuts, egusi, dried mushrooms, and dried fish. As a day student in CCAST Bambili, he had to take care of himself. Cooking was not one of his strong points but he liked food. The world view of the villagers did not expect men to cook even as small boys living with their mothers. He had always enjoyed the food cooked by his mother and was in the habit of criticising the food cooked by the other women in the compound. His mother had always warned him not to say such things especially since the children of the compound were used to eating in any woman's house if invited. Moreover they did not even need to be invited. As long as

181

they were present when the food was ready they were given some to eat.

When he had to go to form one and start living alone and providing food for himself, his mother was worried. The excitement of going away to school did not give allowance for him to think about how he was going to get food. His mother understood this very well and had provided as much as she could to tempt him into cooking. All the food items his mother thought he would need in school to prepare soup was stuffed with his clothes and the bag was heavy too. One needed much energy to carry such a load, walk and talk at the same time, but he had to answer.

'Because of the dust mother.'

They lapsed into silence. They had been moving for more than one hour and the main road leading to the town of Ndop was nowhere in sight. They moved along the path, their footsteps deadened by the thick layer of dust. The morning dew was heavy on the dusty grasses which whipped against their legs as they moved along.

'What about the dust?' Mami Milia asked.

Explaining this would take time and energy and Lientueh wanted to avoid this. It was not unusual for a question to be left unanswered in companionable silence. They walked on.

They had got up at the first cock's crow to assemble all he had to take to school. They had passed five homesteads where the families were still in their huts. As they passed they could hear movements within. Lientueh remembered how for the past weeks they too had been up early preparing to go to the farm. Life in the village was not easy, he had come to realise after two years in secondary school, but once one got used to the rhythm, it no longer looked tedious.

Lientueh looked at the huts as they passed. They walls were of dried mud blocks that produced dust. The roofs were of dried grass that had accumulated dust over the years. There was dust everywhere. The beginning of the farming season was dominated by dust. The ridges on the farms were heaps of dry earth. The clothes they wore to the farm had assumed the colour of dust, and neither the colour nor the texture of these clothes was identifiable. It was normal that clothes had their uses and those for the farms were special.

Each time Lientueh came back from the farm he took time to put water into his nostrils and blow it out to get rid of the dust that had accumulated there as he tilled the dry earth making it porous for the coming rains. The noise he made irritated his mother but she did not complain. He was a college boy and college boys knew how to take care of their bodies more than village boys. Lientueh took a bath every day, village boys did not. His mother had remarked on this. Now he wanted to tease his mother on the phenomenon of nose blowing.

'Mama, do you know why I put water into my nose and blow it out?'

'How can I know?'

''If I do not blow the dust out it will get into my head and block it. When I read my books I will not understand what I read.'

Mami Milia was always concerned with whatever had to do with her son's education or performance at school. He had always been among the first three in class by order of merit since Form One and this pleased her. She believed that her son was going to be a big man in future. She strongly believed in this.

'That is good.' She observed. 'Thank God that there is not much dust in your school like the one we have here, but you had to wash your shirt.'

'Mama I have told you that I will wash it in school. The dust we have in school is the same like the one we have here but the water is cleaner.'

'Is it the dust that makes the water here dirty?' Mami Milia asked.

'Lientueh could not understand why his mother was asking such a question. There was all evidence that the water in the ponds in the raffia bushes were not clean.

One evening they were sitting by the fire waiting for supper to get ready and he had told his mother that drinking dirty water could make you sick. His mother had looked at him with eyes that said 'these children of today, bookwork will turn them into something else.', but it was this something else that she wanted her child to become. She had thought that if the water had to make any one sick, it should be her, let her son be spared. It could not be her because she had drunk the water all her life and she has not been sick. Her son too had drank the water, but she was afraid that too much book would make her son's stomach to be soft for the germs in the water and her son would be sick. She was consoled by the fact that the more book he learnt the less time he would spend in the village.

'Mother, why do you eat lumps of soil you pull from the walls? It is not good'

Mami Milia did not respond, but she thought about it. She did not really know why she ate the soil. She knew that her son was not going to leave her alone if she did not give him an answer. She had to say something.

'I eat it because it has a good taste.'

'A good taste? Lientueh wondered aloud. 'Does soil have a taste?

This was just the type of situation mami Milia wanted to avoid. Her son's incessant questions tired her, though she knew that all he wanted was to know. On the farm while they worked, some of his questions had made her to laugh, thus releasing some of the stress of farm work, but now with this heavy bag on her head, thinking of a suitable answer to give him was tedious

'Eh, mami?' Lientueh prompted. A sudden thought came into her head.

'Remember that you once told me that you enjoy the smell of dust when the first rains fall. Why do you enjoy it?

'Yes I enjoy it but that one is flavour not taste'

In the mother tongue the expression for taste and flavour is the same. Mami milia pondered for a while. What was the difference? She wondered. When you put something nice in your mouth or smell something it was the same. She remembered how her father used to enjoy smoking his pipe. It was the smoke he enjoyed not the tobacco itself. Was it not the same thing? All that went into the mouth or nose had taste

'What goes into your nose or into your mouth has taste.' Mami Milia concluded

Lientueh wanted to laugh and tell his mother that that was not what his teacher had told him. The sense of taste was different from the sense of smell, but his attention was caught by a concentrated haze of dust in the horizon. He did not want to be tempted to feel relieved that it was the dust trail of a moving vehicle. They were now on a small hill from where the surrounding undulating landscape lay spread out for as far as the eye could see. The early morning mist was heavy with particles of dust and made visibility uncertain.

'Mother, it looks as if a vehicle is coming. I have seen dust in the air over there that looks like it is caused by a moving vehicle'

'It cannot be. Today is not a market day. Vehicles cannot come this early.'

Lientueh was disappointed. He would have preferred to be left with the illusion that a vehicle was approaching. Then he realized that if indeed it was a vehicle, it would have passed before they arrived at the main road. Moreover, a vehicle would be a long way away before the dust rose to a level at which it could be seen from far away.

'We have to wait under the mango tree' Lientueh observed. If we knew we would have left later in order not to wait for long.

'It is better to move in the morning when places are still cool and the dust still heavy with dew. When the sun is hot, the dust becomes dry and the wind blows it into your eyes'

Lientueh saw reason in this explanation and kept quiet.

They were approaching the main road and the sight of the mango tree which stood where the path joined the main road was a welcomed sight. It meant that the bags will soon be off their heads and their legs would rest. He would have time to sir under the mango tree and wonder. The mango tree with its thick foliage was like a companion to him. Underneath was always cool even at midday when the sun was very hot. Even the earth under the tree was cool to the touch. Because of the strategic position of this tree, from its location one could see any vehicle coming up from the valley. From the shade it provided, the villagers had made benches of bamboo which were attached to the tree. Here the villagers would sit and wait for vehicles going to the town of Ndop on non-market days. Surrounding the tree in the grasses were evidences of this wait. Groundnut shells, dry corn husks, sugar cane chaff and the occasional plastic paper were littered in the grass. Lientueh found it strange that the area under the tree was always clean and wondered who swept it.

They were now sitting under the tree and waiting. Their necks were relieved of the heavy bags, their legs from the strain of walking and their bodies were resting.

While Lientueh rested his mind was busy. On ordinary days, that is days which were not market days the bread van which came from Ndop to supply bread to the surrounding villages was the only means of transportation to Ndop from where it was easy to get a vehicle to Bambili and Bamenda. The van supplied bread every two days from the market day and it was important for those intending to travel to Ndop, Bambili or Bamenda to know these days else their waiting would be in vain. For a moment Lientueh was tempted to think that they had missed the day. They had been waiting for almost half an hour with no sign of a vehicle coming or its droning sound in the distance.

'What is the day of today?' Lientueh asked.

'Today is Nquitonh. It is the third day from the market day.'

'I thought we had missed the day the bread van comes'

Mami Milia did not respond. She was sitting in her favourite position. Her head was resting on the tree trunk and her legs were stretched out in front of her, with her hands folded over her stomach. Her ankles and toes were covered with dust. The slippers she wore were discoloured by the dust that had seeped into the material from which it was made over the years. No amount of washing could get it to its original colour. He then looked at his sandals. These were the sandals he wore to class. He had worn them because he was most comfortable in them. He wore them more often than he did his other pair of sandals. He wore the other pair when he had no choice.

On his way to school one morning the strap of his regular pair, his old reliable, as he called it had cut. He had to go back home and wear the other one. His 'old reliable' had cut at two points, at his ankle and at the point against which his outer toe pressed. These points had beet stitched with twine which was originally white but which had now become brown blending with the colour of the sandals.

Mami Milia was not anxious or worried. She had the phenomenal patience of villagers to whom time was determined by what went on from sunrise to sunset. Time was not determined by seconds, minutes or hours; it just flowed on with one activity merging into the other. The length of time these activities took did not matter. It was their completion that mattered. They had arrived at the main road, which was what mattered. Now they were waiting for the bread van. That was what mattered.

From his mother's posture Lientueh knew that his mother was not sleeping. Her eyes were closed but she was not sleeping. She was in that state of being where the darkness of the world caused by the closing of the eyes led to the darkness of the mind to the physical things but not to the psychological ones. He often wondered what went on in his mother's mind at such times.

He had also noticed this darkness of the mind on traditional Sundays when no one went to the farm for it was forbidden. She would sit on a log outside the hut and stare at the ground or at the entrance of the compound. Many times he had noticed that although she looked at the entrance of the compound she did not see what was happening there. He had once asked her if she had seen the goats that had walked in a single file into the compound. The sight had attracted him because of the order in which they had walked into the compound. It was like a procession of father mother and children, but Mami Milia had seen nothing.

On such days his step brothers and sisters would be running and playing round the compound. He was an only child and felt that it was just right for him to keep his mother company, but often he could not resist the temptation of joining the others. His mother never prevented him from doing so. Often when he had rushed back to her to ask her about something or to draw her attention to something that had been going on, she would react as if she had been sleeping. He would look into her eyes and the vacant look he saw there confused and worried him

But today he knew that she was not sleeping. He had not seen that vacant look in her eyes when occasionally she opened them. Each time the day of his departure from the village was approaching his mother was more at peace. He often heard her say 'Thank God you will soon go'. Lientueh had always wondered what caused this change of mood meant. He wondered but could not rest the way his mother was doing. His mind wandered. His eyes wandered too. He looked between the bamboos of the bench and saw ants moving in and out of their hole. They were the brown harmless type that made up small anthills as they dug holes into the soil. They were carrying small lumps of soil and depositing them outside. Their activity captivated his interest. He straightened his body on the length of the bench and peered between the bamboo stems. He now clearly saw what they were doing. Some earth had fallen and blocked the passage to their boroughs and they were busy clearing the passage way. The manner in which they scurried to and fro carrying little lumps of earth and the order in which they deposited them at the base of a small mound formed a small one sided pyramid. The distance from the entrance of the hole to the base of the pyramid was about two inches but as Lientueh watched them it seemed as if it was a long distance. The small path was well trodden and smooth. No dust rose as the ants went about their work. As he looked at the ants his thoughts wandered. He envied the ants and their dustless environment. The roads leading into the village and those within the village were always dusty in the dry season and muddy in the wet season. Living in the homesteads one was always aware of the dust. It is made even more menacing when there is a dust storm. The dust on the main road was made worse when the public works department carried out their sporadic grading of the roads. When this happened it was easier for vehicles to move but hell for the villagers. They had to move ankle deep in the dust and inhale the dust when a vehicle passed by. When they blew out phlegm it came out in a thick mushy lump. By the time the passengers in a vehicle arrived their destination they looked like moving corpses dug out of a dusty hole with their eyes as the only sign of life. The roads had just been graded and this was the situation in the village.

Lientueh's thoughts moved from the smooth path of the ants to the dusty roads. The result was that he dozed off briefly. In the world of his brief unconsciousness he found himself riding on a smooth well tarred road. Something hung round him like white dust but it did not come from the road. It was not churned up by the tyres of the vehicle. It just slipped passed him as he rode by. The wind that blew into his face was cool and clean. He inhaled it and felt good. He felt at home being driven on this road. He felt as if he was part of this road. He felt as if he had brought the road into existence. He felt proud as he rode along, the vehicle gathering speed as his spirits rose. His body felt relaxed and he felt almost comfortable. He was drifting...

The vehicle came to an abrupt stop and the impact shook him. He came awake. His mother was shaking him gently. A cool breeze was rustling through the leaves of the mango tree and brought a welcomed coolness beneath it.

The sun was overhead now and the surrounding landscape sizzled with the heat. Looking at the horizon and at the sky there was no sign of a wind but the breeze could be felt. What actually betrayed its presence was the rustling of the leaves overhead and the faint trail of the dust in the distance. It was certainly dust from the trail of a vehicle. It was thicker, it was not like the type raised by a dust storm which whirls and carries along debris. This one was consistently brown. The ubiquitous dust haze had disappeared as the moisture trapped in the dust evaporated and the dust could now be blown away. Any one waiting for a vehicle by the roadside on a dusty road knew from experience that the height of the dust trail determined how near the vehicle was. With the light wind blowing, the dust was scattered faster than when there was no wind. The dust trail they were looking at hung just above the shrubs. The vehicle was near.

Vehicles plying the roads between villages were adapted in a skilful manner. Whatever the make of the vehicle it was always adapted to carry more than its original capacity. The approaching vehicle had been a regular van for transporting goods. A third of its body work had been removed and a carriage higher than the height of the vehicle added. On the top of the remaining two thirds of the vehicle another carriage had been attached. The carriage behind could take eight people sitting closely together. The other carriage at the top was for luggage. In this way the van served two purposes.

The driver of the van was such a jolly fellow and had established such a strong bond with the villagers that even on market days they preferred his van to the buses that came from Bamenda. After all they were still packed like sardines in a can just as the van driver did. The buses were also so old that dust seeped in through the cracks and crevices in the body work. They arrived at their destination equally covered with dust. The preferred the dust and a driver who joked with them than the dust with a driver who did not respect them nor was concerned about their luggage.

Mami Milia rushed to the road side and stood watching. As soon as the van appeared she started waving for it to stop. She did not really have to, for the driver of the van knew that people from that neighbourhood travelling to Ndop town always waited under this mango tree. There were days when he arrived at this spot with all the available space behind occupied, but villagers never believed that a vehicle could be full. They thought there was always space. Just telling them was not enough. He had to stop to let them see for themselves. There were times he had to convince them by letting them try to get into a sitting position by themselves. When the other passengers complained how uncomfortable they were then the insistent party would get out amidst grumbling from those already seated. While this is going on the driver would make fun of the incapacity of his van to carry all the villagers. Without allowing anybody to get really annoyed he had made his point and would drive away assuring those left behind of the certainty of his carrying them the next time.

The van slowed down and stopped. Today was a bad day for the driver and a good one for the passengers on board and those about to come on board for there was sitting space for everyone. If this had been the contrary then Lientueh and his mother would have waited in vain. There were just six people behind. More to this he was not going to sit on the extended tailboard of the van which bounced and galloped at every little pothole. The driver jumped down

'Ah Mami Milia' he called. He had this knack of knowing people by name. 'You have come to send your husband off to school. That is very good.'

'Yes she replied. 'We thought you were not going to come today. We have been here since morning'

'Ashia, you know that today is Mamfung Market and I had to go right there to sell bread before coming back. On the way one of my tyres gave way and I had to stop and have it repaired. I hope I will get to Ndop with it. My spare is too bad to be repaired in a hurry. If it gives way then I have to take both to Ndop to repair before coming back. You know what that means.'

'God forbid that that should happen' Mami Milia answered. When such a misfortune met a driver the passengers would have to wait for about an hour or two for the driver to get to Ndop repair the tyres and come back. It is easier today with motor taxis carrying people within and without the villages.

As the driver spoke he helped Mami Milai carry the bags to the carriage at the back of the van.

There was cargo on the carriage at the top of the van but it was not yet full. The back of the van was also not full so there was no need to send the bags up.

All this while, Lientueh looked at the hooded figures sitting at the back of the van. They had covered themselves up with loincloths to protect their clothing from the dust. He too was going to do same. As he looked he did not like what he saw. He wished it could be different. The driver after placing the bags in such a way that they could not fall off, turned to go and caught this look on the boy's face. He said, 'Young man, I see you do not like this dust. It is good that you are going to school. Read your books well and become an engineer in future. You will tar our roads and we will not suffer from the dust like this. If I had the chance to go to school, I would not have been a driver.'

With this said he walked to driver's side of the van, opened the door and got in. He had not spoken out of indignation. He had seen something in the boy's eyes which had transmitted a message to him. It was the hope of every villager that one day the government would have pity on them and tar this road. This was one of the major roads that linked the North West Province to the western Province, yet it was left in such a deplorable state.

Lientueh climbed into the carriage behind, wrapped the loincloth which his mother had given him on his body, even covering his head with it, and waited for the vehicle to take off. He did not say good bye to his mother. He was pondering on what the driver had said. Mami Milia on her part had also been touched by what the man had said. It had always been her dream for her son to become a big man and work in a big office in Bamenda or even in Yaounde. It had never occurred to her that it was not the big people who actually made the roads, but she knew that they were the ones who decided where and when the roads were to be constructed.

The parliamentarian for their area on one of his rare visits to the village had promised them that this particular road was going to be tarred. This had evoked a roar of applause from the people. It was now five years and nothing had changed. As Mami Milia walked back home, with her steps bringing up little puffs of dust as her slippers slapped and raised them she was confused. She did not know what to wish for her son. She had always wanted her son to be a big man but what the driver had said intrigued her. She did not know which was better, a big man or an engineer. The parliamentarian who had promised them the road was a big man but he had lied. She had the feeling that all the big men who came to speak to them in the village about the government were all liars. She did not want her son to become a liar. She saw how these big men suddenly became rich as soon as they got these big posts. She wanted her son to be an honest man and to help the village with this problem of the road. If being an engineer would make him that, whatever an engineer was, then she was wishing her son would one day be an engineer.

The Cocoa Boys

The cocoa boys were around again. There was going to be action. The usually quiet Muyenge village with its farmers going to the farms as early as five am and coming back at one o clock in the afternoon now had more to do at home. Instead of sitting at the front of their homes as they used to do when they came back from the farms bare-chest because of the heat, they now had more to do at home. The cocoa beans had to be dried and sorted out. Those who did not have tons of cocoa beans did the sorting and drying by themselves but those who had tons and tons of them employed seasonal workers. This was the season when such workers flooded the village and changed the lifestyle of the people for a while. There were more mouths to feed so the food sellers were in business. There were also many more incidents of theft as the desire to get many more bags of cocoa was in the hearts of those who wanted to make fast money. The young girls too who thought they could make a few tens of thousands from their bodies were excited. It was the cocoa season and all business was brisk.

It was the month of November, the peak of the cocoa season. Money was flowing and everybody wanted a share. The seasonal workers who worked on contract splitting cocoa pods and transporting the beans to the drying barns wanted a share. The women selling food by the road side were already in business. The 'buyam sellams' of foodstuff were already around for it was the dry season and the roads were passable again. Even the small boys and girls with buckets of snails made in soya form and accra balls in trays had bought new rubber shoes to brave the rocks and they moved in the neighbourhood advertising their ware 'Slow guys! Slow guys. 'Hot Koki Hot koki di go! Fine accra di go!

Epiene, alias 'Big Boy' and his gang were sitting in a makeshift restaurant in the heart of Muyenge village which had suddenly developed an aspect of a township. They were not really a gang in the real sense of the word. They were called men who bought cocoa for a Licensed Buying Agent [LBA] resident in Muyuka. The LBA'S were the intermediaries between the cocoa farmers and the exporters. The LBA's in turn had men who went into the hinterlands to buy the cocoa for them. They were looked upon as a gang because they were always together except when business required one or two of them to be away.

Their master had a ware house in Muyenge where the cocoa was kept before transportation to Muyuka and eventually to Douala. A small section of it had been converted into sleeping quarters. Jute bags in which the cocoa seeds were put weighed, sealed and transported made up the beds and nails on the walls for shirts to be hung completed the furnishings of the sleeping quarters. One might think that the cocoa boys lived a hard life but to them it was fun, excitement and money- plenty of money. There were times of tension when they faced stiff competition from other buyers of cocoa. There were times of frustration when they could not meet up with the number of cocoa bags they were expected to buy. This happened often in the low season of the cocoa harvest which occurs in the months of April and May.

Business was done to maximise profit. A sort of non-written agreed monopoly was practiced. The prizes of basic commodities increased in Muyenge village not because of any increase in prizes nationwide but because of the sudden high demand. Cooked food in particular became very expensive. After all the seasonal workers had to buy food or starve for everybody was trying to make as much money as possible during this period.

Epiene was eating beans and puff puff with a cup of tea beside his plate. A ball of puff puff was twenty five francs. It was not much larger than what was formally sold for ten francs. Flour had become expensive but this was not the reason. Everybody wanted to make the best of the influx of people and the increase in the flow of cash. This was an exciting period and they would all go back to the daily labouring on the farms when this season is over.

Epiene held the plate with his large hands as he used the last piece of puff puff to clean the beans sauce from the plate. His large hands had gained him the name bog boy. He had been known by this name since he was in the primary school. During a quarrel with a boy bigger than him he had given the boy a slap and he had fallen down. Instead of calling him big hands which would have sounded insulting, his friends just called him 'big boy'. He liked lukewarm tea in the morning. It was too hot to drink hot tea. He loved the taste of sugar and milk, especially the condensed milk which was thick in consistency and sweet. When he lifted the cup only one of his fingers could enter the space between the handle of the cup and its body. A second finger could not enter. The smell of fried eggs from a nearby breakfast corner assailed his nostrils. He could have eaten a plate of the fried eggs. He had the money but thought it would be extravagant to do so today. On the days he drank tea and ate bread it was usually accompanied by a plate of four fried eggs. It was his dictum that the body that worked the money should profit from the money. He had discovered that bread and tea with egg was too light a breakfast for the type of job he did.

Molongo alias ' Slow Guy' was sitting next to him. He had been given that name because of his love for snails. Whether snails were made in the form of soya, fried or cooked with the eru vegetable or in njangsa sauce, Molongo enjoyed it. His favourite was the Soya type which the children carried around in transparent plastic buckets. Wherever these children with their buckets of snails saw him, they lingered around waiting to see if he was going to call any of them. A story is told of how he and his friends ate a whole bucket of snails that contained about thirty sticks of snail soya.

Molongo was the life wire of the group. He assured the sanity and stability of members of the group by ensuring that each of them had a fair share of the extra profits they made. Each of them was paid a certain amount of money depending on the number of cocoa bags they bought. This was important because they were not the only cocoa buyers in Muyenge. There were many others both groups and individuals and the competition was stiff. If any action was to be carried out Molongo made sure that none of them drank any beer that day or that evening. In fact he made sure that none of them got drunk enough to babble any of the clandestine activities. Though Epiene, alias Big Boy was the official head of the group Molongo was the unofficial head. He directed their unofficial activities and no one complained. At the end of each of their buying expedition when they had to go back to Muyuka, every statistic of the number of bags of cocoa that had been bought and the amounts at which they had been bought were well calculated and signed. In fact every doctoring of the documents had to be carefully done. This was the duty of the official leader. Molongo was in charge of the extra bags of cocoa they came up with. He made sure that the bags of cocoa got to Kumba.

Across the bench on which their plates of food were placed were Joe Smiler and Kola. Joe Smiler was the fun man, not that he made fun, he just looked funny. The shape of his lips gave the impression that he was perpetually smiling. He was quick tempered and the supposed smile on his face made people to take him for granted or for his acquaintances to make an inadvertent joke on his looks thinking he was going to take it light-heartedly. His angry outburst often took them by surprise. They usually retracted with apologies or shrugged and walked away. Kola on his part cannot be qualified. He was just Kola, quiet and obtrusive. People often looked at him as a misfit in the group, but he had something which the group needed. He had strength and cunning. What they did on the side to make extra money needed strength, stamina and cunning. Kola slight of build with a protruding back of the head had all of these. As they ate his head was bent over the plate of beans and puff puff to which had been added some fried ripe plantains. He drank water. Tea made him drowsy in the heat. He soon finished the plate of beans and puff puff. There was a bowl of pap in front of him. He held a ball of puff puff in his right hand while he lifted spoonfuls of pap into his mouth with his left hand. He was left handed and a jab with his left hand in the course of a fight often sent his opponent to the ground.

The cocoa boys had been in Muyenge village for two weeks and were approaching the end of the third week. The bright November morning sun was getting hot. It was always hot in Muyenge village. Located on the leeward side of the Buea Mountain there was not a breath of wind to bring down the temperature. Whether walking, working or just sitting, one sweated. Sweating had become part of their daily lives and the villages no longer paid attention to it. Sweat was already forming on Epiene's forehead as he ate. His armpit was damp. He always wore a short sleeve singlet to absorb the sweat. He did not like to wear sleeveless singlets which left his armpits exposed and allowed sweat to trickle down his sides.

The main street that ran through the town was busy. To call it a street is an over statement. What identified it as a street were the two rows of houses that bordered it, the number of people moving up and down it, the number of provision stores, makeshift restaurants and motor taxis, popularly known as 'bensikin' or 'okada' that carried people in and out of the village. The street was as rocky as any other part of the village.

Grading the street was out of the question. The rocks were not only on the surface, some went deep into the soil. The whole area rested on a deposit of lava from the Buea Mountain. The drivers plying the road from Muyuka through Owe to Muyenge knew the road very well. They knew were the outcroppings of the rocks were and avoided them. These were dangerous as a sudden knock on the underneath of the vehicle would burst a vital connection in the mechanism and either water, oil, petrol or break fluid would start leaking out. There were other parts of the road which had no rocks. These were slippery in the rainy season and dusty in the dry season, but the road passing through Muyenge village was all rocky.

The centre of the village is situated on an elevation which gave it prominence. With no electricity, the two or three generators owned by bar owners lit up this area. It was a beacon of light to the rest of the village and the country side at night. The other streets had nothing but hurricane lamps lighting them up like glow worms in the dark

In addition to the men whip had flocked into Muyenge village to increase the labour force in the cocoa harvest, a new phenomenon was taking place among the 'buyam sellams.'

These women used to come only on market days and buy foodstuff to retail in nearby towns, but some of the women had been coming from as far as Douala to buy foodstuff. These did not come only on market days. They would come on a market day and stay for many more days going right to the farms to negotiate and buy directly from there. Since this freed the farmer from the task of harvesting and carrying to the market, they sold at relatively cheap prizes. Eventually prizes on market days were increased.

Life in Muyenge village at this time of the year was a show. It was a money grabbing show, a show in dexterity of cheating and lying. For the young girls it was a time to show off their God-given wares to get the richest arrivals. It was a show of fighting and drinking in bars. Epiene and his gang were part of the show, but the exciting part of their own show was clandestine.

'We should start putting things together today' Epiene addressed his partners when they had left the eating spot and were standing by the roadside.

'We are still waiting for the truck from Bai-Gras and Kuke Mbomo. When we see the number of bags of cocoa from there and it completes our demand then we can prepare to leave at the end of the week' Molongo explained.

As they were talking a truck drove passed them. It was loaded with bags of cocoa and lurched as it crawled over the rocks on the road. It was the truck they had been waiting for.

They were happy. If things went well they might even leave before the end of the week.

With full stomachs they move towards the ware house. The truck was in front of them. These were four happy young men who loved what they were doing and took life as it came. Joe Smiler had not spent the night in the warehouse with the others and Big Boy was anxious to know what had happened

'So how was it?' He asked turning to Joe Smiler.

'How was what, Joe Smiler asked. Big Boy looked at the others. They were all smiling but secretly looking away as if they had not heard Big Boy's question. If any of them spent the night out it was with a girl. They had agreed that it was important for the others to know where each of them could be found if they had to go off for something private. If any of them spent the night out when they were on a buying trip then it was with a girl. Joe Smiler hardly spent the night out. So when he had announced the previous evening that he was going to spend the night out the others had been curious.

'The night' Big Boy pursued.

'It was dark and hot' Joe responded. The others busted out laughing.

'You are a cocoa boy. I am sure it was worth the cocoa boys you spent' Joe Smiler smiled. He actually smiled.

'You want me to talk about it?' he asked

'Yes', the answer came in a chorus.

'No I will not.'

'At least show her to us.' Slow Guy jokingly pleaded.

'So that you should take her away from me? Joe asked.

Bog Boy and Slow Guy roared with laughter. Kola only smiled. He had come to understand and accept the fact that what Bog Boy and Slow Guy did and said was not out of malice spite or meanness. They were just what they were. Kola was drawn to Smiler who did not talk as much as the others did. The unwritten code of ethics among the four was unshakable. They accepted and tolerated each other's idiosyncrasies. It was accepted and understood that once any of them showed interest in a girl the others should keep off. Quarrels over girls were known to be the cause of divisions and betrayals among men who were together for a common interest. There is no man who feels as angry betrayed and who is as vindictive as a man whose girlfriend or wife has left him for his friend. This could not happen among the coco boys.

The cocoa boy Big Boy had referred to had a different meaning. The expression 'cocoa boy' was also used to refer to the ten thousand francs note which had the picture of a cocoa pod on it. This expression was also used to refer to the men who came to Muyenge at this time of the year with wads of ten thousand franc notes tucked in their trouser or coat pockets. The money was for business but some also went for pleasure.

Big Boy and his partners were cocoa boys. They were young men who had money and were ready to spend it. Everybody was attracted by money, especially the young girls who were on holiday. Among the women there was a sort of unacknowledged price control. They knew from which men to ask for five thousand francs and from which to ask for ten thousand francs. For Big boy and his gang it was always ten thousand francs or more depending on how far the relationship had gone and they were also young and demanding.

Asking about how the night had been spent was nothing unusual. What was there to hide? The 'Calabout' houses had thin wooden walls and sometimes with holes where white ants had eaten away the wood. There were no ceiling to allow the free circulation of air and it was possible to move from one room to the other through the rafters so did the sounds. The creaking of the bed and the shrieks or groans of those involved in the action could be heard in the next room. Any one curious enough could even see the action through the holes or cracks in the walls.

The four men arrived at the warehouse and met the driver with the two men they had seen in the truck. They did not know them.

'How de waka bi dey?' Big Boy asked. He did not look at the two men. He looked at the driver's face. He did not like what he saw there.

'Eh bi bad, oga.' The driver replied. Big Boy's heart sank. He was afraid that the driver must have gotten into trouble, for the truck could not be full with cocoa bags and the driver was saying that the journey was bad.

'Weti you mean? Big Boy asked.

' Make this cocoa enter house first then I go tell you.'

One of the two men turned to big Boy and said' Plenty de coca na we own.'

'Yes', the driver interrupted him. 'a wan move de one for here then a go take wuna own for wuna place'

The rest of the three men just watched. This was Big Boy's responsibility and the others could intervene only when it was necessary. For now none of them knew what had happened.

Each time a truck full of cocoa passed to a warehouse, young boys followed to carry the bags from the trucks to the warehouse. Five of them had arrived and were waiting to be directed on what to do. Usually the driver knew the number of bags and estimated how many each boy was to carry. They were paid fifty francs per bag. The experienced carriers were assigned fifty bags each and the inexperienced ones twenty five bags each. Carrying fifty kilos of dead weight on the back was not an easy thing to do. If you were not strong enough or if the bag was placed at a certain angle there would be dislocation of the spine. When the owner of the cocoa wanted the work to be done quickly he assigned each of the boys twenty five bags and got more boys to do the work. The bags of cocoa were not many so Big boy got four of the boys to carry twenty five bags each. The truck had the capacity for three hundred bags. Only one hundred of the bags on the truck belonged to Big boy.

When all was done the driver drove away with the two men. Big boy sat on a bench that leant on the wall of the ware house and waited. Seeing his mood the others went quietly into the warehouse, into the sleeping quarters and lay down on the jute bags. Big boy was good at talking but when he was faced with a problem or when he was angry he kept quiet.

Their estimated number of cocoa for their two- week stay in Muyenge was 800 to 1000 bags. They usually ended up with 1100 to 1200 bags, sometimes even 1250 bags. Whatever extra bags they could get with the amount of money they were given was theirs, but the books were always doctored to reflect the right figures.

As the three men lay on the bags they said nothing to each other. They had not made their target number of bags and they were expected back in Muyuka at the end of the week. Their master would wait for them in Muyuka to make sure that the right number of cocoa bags was going to Douala and that the trucks were being driven by reliable drivers. He would have his number of bags of cocoa but if this happens it would drastically reduce what they had gotten for themselves. This was a crucial season. They needed extra money to do the things they wanted to do. It would soon be Christmas. They had already taken money to supply two hundred bags of cocoa to another LBA in Kumba. Arrangements had been made for the cocoa to be carried to Kumba.

There were many intermediaries in the cocoa trade. To trace the source of any bags of cocoa was almost impossible because at each level the cocoa beans from one bag, for example, was mixed with beans from other bags and put in another bag

This trip was going to be a difficult one. They had not met their target number of bags. Something had to be done and done fast. When the driver came back, Big boy did not allow him to catch his breath as he jumped down from the driver's seat.

'wetin happen?'

'Oga a no see cocoa'

'why'

'a se a no see cocoa'

'You bi go fo carri cocoa no fo fianam'

'Cocoa no bi de fo carriyam'

'Why?' Big boy was getting exasperated. He was also beginning to imagine what had happened but he wanted to hear what the driver had to say.

'De boys them se de work no bi waka. Dem se de fine cocoa de no siyam'

Big boy understood that something had gone wrong. It was not the driver's fault. He had been sent to carry cocoa not to buy. Every arrangement had been made with the farmers from whom they bought cocoa. Arrangements had also been made with some boys who sold cocoa on the open market. These were the boys who raided the cocoa drying barns at night and sold cocoa at a cheaper prize.

'Okay wusa de money fo dat cocoa we you cariyam?'

The man searched his pockets and brought out two ten thousand franc notes.

Big boy was now angry.

'You carri two hundred bags for 20 000 frs?' How you foolish so? Yo no know se for cari cocoa came for Muyenge na 200 frs for one bag?'

'Oga, eh no bi fine o! Mi a bi di come back wit empty motor. A mit dis people fo cona road. Dem se them get cocoa for bringam for Muyenge. A se if I deny I go loss 20.000frs an I go come back here wit empty moto. So I carriyam. Dis one fit buy petrol.

Big boy calmed down. There was no use getting angry over such a trifle. There were more crucial things to worry about. He folded the money and put it in his trouser pocket. It was generally believed that whatever money any one handed over after an errand was not the exact money received. Big boy gave the driver nothing.

The driver an older person to Big boy did not take offence. In the cocoa business what was respected was money, the cocoa boys. Respect for human beings did not come into it. It was not unusual for a young boy to bully and even humiliate an elder person just because he worked for his father

People working for each LBA were like members of a family. It was a chain from the cocoa farmer from the interior villages to the men who moved from village to village buying cocoa, to the drivers who carried the cocoa bags out of the villages, to those who selected the cocoa beans putting them into bags of fifty and a hundred kilos. To leave one LBA to work for another without a very good reason was looked upon as betrayal.

Big boy and his gang had become part of the family of workers who worked for Mr. Kosa. He trusted them. They were hard working and he had never seen anything wrong with the entries in the ledger or receipts they presented. They always brought the quantity of cocoa he wanted, in time and good quality too. For all of these they were hard working and honest. They delivered the goods and were well paid. The thrill was in the kickbacks they made. Mr. Kosa never knew of these. Now the thrill was being threatened. They were in a dilemma. Something had to be done and done fast. Whenever they found themselves in such a situation they knew what to do. They had done it many times before and all was fine in the end.

Big boy and his gang were well known in the countryside around Muyenge village. They were the cocoa boys in both sense of the word. They were ruthless and aggressive in their buying strategies, but they paid promptly before or after collecting the cocoa. The farmers liked them for this. There were times when they met more cocoa than they had budgeted for. These they took and paid later.

Not all the cocoa farmers were attached to licensed buyers. Those not attached sold in the open market. These were the people who made it possible for people like Big boy and his gang to make high kickbacks.

Before the harvesting season many contracts had been made. Many farmers were not able to purchase the insecticides that were necessary for the healthy flowering and eventual formation of the cocoa pods. It was common practice for the licensed buyers to supply the farmers with cans of insecticide in return for a number of bags of cocoa commensurate to the cost of the numbers of cans taken. The black pod fungi could destroy a whole plantation as the wind and the insects carry the pores around.

The presence or sign of this fungus on a pod was cause for alarm as the pores could also be blown from one plantation to another. So it was imperative for the plantations to be sprayed. This was what ensured a good harvest. This type of contract also attracted exploitation as the number of bags of cocoa did not depend on the fluctuating cost of insecticide and cost of a kilo of cocoa.

The weighing machines were also owned by the licensed buyers. The big names like Mr. Kosa owned some of the machines located in the surrounding villages of Kuke Mbomo, Bia Gras and Bova. Smaller buying agents weighed their cocoa there for a price. The weighing machines had been adjusted in such a way that 55 kilos of cocoa weighed as 50 kilos. For every ten bags measured there was an extra bag. This was not evident at the buying points, When the bags were brought to Muyenge they rearranged and weighed, put in fifty kilogram bags before transportation to Muyuka. This was another way in which Big boy and his gang made extra money.

Occasionally they were contacted by boys who had cocoa to sell. With these boys there was no time to weigh the cocoa. They collected the money and delivered the cocoa. They had to make sure that the cocoa beans were good. Such dealings were very delicate because any disagreement between the parties would lead to both parties being exposed or jungle justice would be used to settle the problem. Before the driver was sent to carry the cocoa Mulongo had made the necessary arrangements for some boys to supply them with twenty five bags of cocoa. With this arrangement they were sure to get 100 bags of cocoa of their own. But they had failed to do so. When the driver had arrived at the agreed spot between Kuke Mbomo and Bai Gras, there was no one there. He had sounded the horn of the truck, came down to the hut and knocked at the door. There was no response. He went round to the back of the hut. As he looked round, one of the boys emerged from the bushes and informed him that they had not been able to get the cocoa but was sure to get it in the next two days. There was nothing that he could do but to return to Muyenge with what he had. The driver could not ask for the money that had been given to the boys as advanced payment. That was not his job. All he had to do was to transport cocoa to Muyenge and he did just that.

Big boy was not worried about the money that had been paid to the boys. He knew that he was either going to get cocoa from them or he was going to get his money whatever happened. What worried him was that they had taken money for a hundred bags of cocoa but had only seventy five bags. They had always kept their promise. Were they not the cocoa boys? They had their reputation to maintain both as expert cocoa buyers with abundant cocoa boys. As they weighed and stitched the bags of cocoa they discussed on what could be done.

Their discussion took them to an incident that had happened two years back. They had been complains about the rampant and mysterious disappearance of bags of cocoa on the way from Muyenge to Muyuka. Many drivers had been accused and embarrassed by this situation. From some trucks, as many as twenty five bags could not be accounted for when the drivers arrived at Muyuka. Nobody had ever solved the problem. They had been suspicions of theft by highway robbers. But the drivers had not been attacked by anybody. It was later suspected that maybe the thieves climbed unto the trucks and pushed down the bags of cocoa. This was possible because drivers and passengers of smaller vehicles had seen a bag or two of cocoa lying by the roadside. But these could have fallen from overloaded lurching vehicles. Nothing specific ever came out to account for the disappearance of bags of cocoa on the way to Muyuka. They still had one truck left. Each truck carried 300 bags of cocoa or a bit more. The 100 extra bags would go to Kumba in another truck. As of date they lacked 15 bags. 10 bags had been sent by the boys who had earlier failed to supply 25 bags.

Big boy and Joe Smiler were sitting in front of a hut smoking. They did not drink much but they smoked. They smoked as they said to keep their minds alert. Down the road Kola was sitting in front of another hut in the outskirts of Ikata Village. This was one of the villages nearest to Muyenge. They had carefully planned the operations of that night. They were sure to accomplish this task. After all 15 bags of cocoa was not a big deal.

It was three a.m. The rumbling of two trucks disturbed the peace of the night. It was a Thursday night and many of the cocoa buyers were already transporting their cocoa bought that week to Muyenge. The last batch would follow the next day Friday and they would go for the weekend to come back on Monday. These trucks were driven at the speed of 20 to 25 kmph. Anything faster would likely send the trucks into the bushes as they bounced over the rocks. Sitting in one of the trucks one could hear the creaks and groans of the body work as it strained under the weight of the cocoa bags and the lurching movement. About a kilometre behind the second truck was a pick up van driven by Slow Guy.

Kola watched the first truck pass by. That would be handled by Big boy and Joe Smiler who were waiting in another hut between Ikata village and Bafia. By the time the second truck passed in front of the hut where Kola was waiting he was already by the roadside. The beams of light from the truck lit the road ahead for about six meters. The sides of the roads were in total darkness. Kola waited. As soon as the truck passed he ran after it and skipped. He gripped the tailboard and hauled himself up unto the cocoa bags. The cocoa bags were not covered because it was the dry season. Kola set to work pushing down the bags of cocoa.

As the truck lurched and swayed, the sound of the engine which had served its master for ten years with just minor repairs roared in exhaustion. The driver's companion had his head leaning backward on the headrest of the seat. His eyes were closed, his mouth open and a small wheezing sound issued from his nostrils as he slept. He had been conversing with the driver to keep awake, but soon succumbed to nature's demand. The driver was alert but all his attention was focused on the road ahead, looking out for protruding rocks and swerving away in time to avoid them. Occasionally he flashed his headlights and dimmed them. This was not to see the road better but just for the exercise of it, for the nature of the road and the speed of the truck required a closer view. He focused on the road and heard nothing.

The decision of the gang had been brewed out of desperation. They were cocoa buyers too and were not in the habit of robbing their colleagues. But desperate times required desperate measures. They needed the money and their reputation was at stake. They had decided to get ten bags from the first truck and five bags from the second truck. This way the loss will be spread.

Kola successfully pushed down ten bags. He jumped down and gave a military salute to the departing truck and the swirling dust that accompanied it and blocked his view. Soon after, the pickup van arrived and loaded the cocoa. He joined Slow Guy in front of truck and they drove on.

They were approaching the next hut where Joe Smiler and Big boy were supposed to have been waiting for the first truck. As they passed they did not see any glowing cigarette ends and knew that they had left. As they drove on Slow Guy thought that he saw a figure in the darkness ahead. At this time of the night it was impossible to see passenger vehicles on this road not to mention individuals on foot. For a moment he thought he was seeing a ghost or one of the witches people often said they saw on this road. He flashed his head lights. The figure was jumping and waving his hands. As he got nearer he noticed that it was a man. He slowed down and saw Joe Smiler. He stopped the pickup in the middle of the road and both of them climbed out.

'What happened?' both of them asked at the same time.

'Come! Come!' Joe Smiler whispered urgently. They followed him into the bushes. In the light of a torch they saw Big Boy lying under a tree. His shirt had been removed and tied round his right hand. It was soaked with blood. Sow Guy and Kola stared in bewilderment.

'What happened?' Slow Guy asked again. The operation that night was his concern. To him for Big Boy to be wounded on his right hand was a disaster. His heart raced. This was trouble. Joe Smiler did not answer. Sloe Guy sat by Big Boy and held his left hand.

'Big Boy, Big Boy can you hear me?' Big Boy turned his head groaned and opened his eyes

'Help me sit up.' He requested. Joe Smiler and Slow Guy helped him to sit and lean against the tree. 'Loosen the shirt' he said. Slow Guy gently undid his shirt. The three middle fingers had been crushed, and bones and flesh hung limply. Blood was rapidly seeping out and dripping unto the ground. Slow Guy cut the chain from his neck and tied Big Boy's wrist. It was so tight that the flow of blood reduced. While Joe Smiler retied the hand with the shirt, Slow Guy went back to the pickup and came back with water in a Tangui bottle and a packet of Paracetamol tablets. He made Big Boy to drink some of the water and swallow two of the tablets, and then he turned and looked at Joe Smiler. He asked no questions but Joe began to explain.

'He climbed on the back of the truck then I saw him falling and shouting'

'Did the truck stop?'

'No, it didn't'

'Did you take the number?'

Joe Smiler did not answer. He found it unnecessary for they all knew the number on the number plate of the truck, its owner and the driver. They sat in silence for a while, each thinking of what to do next. They all had things to say but it was Slow Guy's prerogative to initiate the talking. Something like this had never happened to them. They cheated and outsmarted other buyers. They made money out of people's greed and stupidity. They never thought that they would out rightly steal but the possibility of it was not far from their activities and desires.

The strange disappearance of cocoa bags from trucks at night had been really puzzling to some cocoa transporters. Some like Mr. Quane suspected what was happening. The incidents of the supposedly mysterious disappearance of

216

cocoa had made such an impression on him that he had decided to take some precautions. His trucks never left Muyenge unprotected. It was getting to the end of the week and some of his workers were going back to Muyuka with the cocoa they had bought. One of his trucks had been targeted, but as usual someone was lying on the cocoa bags waiting for any intruder with a cutlass. Big boy had been the intruder and now he needed medical help. Slow Guy concluded.

'We have no choice but to take Big Boy to a hospital'. The others looked at him and said nothing. They wanted him to get to the end of his ideas then they can fill in the gaps. Slow Guy did not like being interrupted or challenged, but all of them knew that they were in real trouble. He continued 'We will drive unto the next village and wait. Early in the morning, Joe You will take a 'bendsiken' with Big Boy and go to Muyuka. Go to a hospital there. Do whatever you can. We will go back to Muyenge and prepare to carry the cocoa we have bought. We will meet you later in the day'

'I cannot take him to a hospital' Slow Guy said when he realised that Slow Guy had finished speaking. Big Boy turned and looked at him.

'Why?' Slow Guy asked. Three pairs of eyes were on Joe Smiler.

Those people in the truck will surely report this incident to the police in Muyuka. If they said that they cut the fingers of one of the boys then the first place they would start looking is in the hospitals and clinics around.

'Yes that is true'. Kola confirmed. Big Boy listened to them and said nothing. He could not believe that this had happened to him. He looked at his bandaged hand and waited for the others to conclude. If their decisions did not appeal to him he would have his say.

'What do you suggest?' Slow Guy asked.

' I think that Big Boy should be taken to a hospital in Buea or Limbe.

These places are not far away and news flies.' Slow Guy argued.

'We can tell a convincing story'

'Like what?' Slow Guy was the master planner and did not like what was happening. He was losing grip.

'We can say that Big Boy works in the oil mill in Mondoni and a piece of iron fell on his hand. That way the hospital people will not link him to cocoa and this incident.'

They all saw the reliability of the suggestion. But Slow Guy was not satisfied. He turned to Big Boy.

'Big Boy do not think that I am not interested in your wellbeing. I just want to make sure that we do not get into more trouble. How do we get you to Buea or Limbe?' Joe Smiler was thinking ahead.

'The bendsiken' that will take us to Muyuka will leave us after the motor park. Then I will come to the motor park and get a bus which will pick him up on the way.'

Kola spoke for the second time.

'He cannot get into a bus with his hand like this'

'I know a nurse in the health centre in Owe village. She will remove this shirt, clean the fingers and bandage them. I will get him another shirt in Owe'.

Joe Smiler's suggestion met with approval.

'What do you think, Big Boy?' Slow Guy asked.

'It is all right with me. I just wonder what you are going to tell our big man in Muyuka.'

'Do not worry. I am going to take care of that.' But Big Boy continued

'Our supply for Kumba is short...' Slow Boy cut in

'It is not much. I am going to handle the situation' Slow Guy did not want to think about cocoa for now. He had better things to think about. Five bags of cocoa less was not the problem.

As Big Boy sat with Joe Smiler at the front of the pickup with Slow Guy at the wheel and Kola on the bags of cocoa behind, each of them was thinking his own thoughts.

Slow Guy saw his plans to display his cocoa boys to the university girls in Buea during the Christmas holidays failing. He had planned to get the coolest chick in Molyko and show those university boys that it is money that speaks, not book. He was sure that Big Boy would love the idea. Both of them had gone on a drinking spree in Kumba last year and it was wonderful. The beer had flowed and the girls were exciting. But what was in vogue this year were university girls. He had heard that they were good and loved cocoa boys. He was going to be there for them.

But now, either Big Boy was going to still be in the hospital by then or he would be without three fingers on his right hand. Which girl would look at such a boy? He needed company for this adventure. Joe Smiler was out of the question. He himself had been amused by his funny looking face when he had first met him, and his quick temper would spoil everything. He wanted to be the coolest guy around and anybody with him had to be equally cool.

Kola was always talking of sending money to his parents. He wanted to build a house for them in the village. Moreover he was very thrifty in the way he spent his money. Slow Guy did not see Kola spending money the way he intended to spend the cocoa boys in Molyko.

Things were falling apart. In his mind Slow Guy saw the disintegration of the most famous cocoa boys in Muyenge.

There was something that helped to keep the cocoa boys together; it was their ability to perform. No cocoa boy could survive without two strong capable hands in the buying of cocoa and what it takes to spend the cocoa boys.